Game of Hearts

Cathy Yardley

Copyright © 2018 by Cathy Wilson

All rights reserved.

No portion of this book may be reproduced in any form without written permission from the publisher or author, except as permitted by U.S. copyright law.

contents

1. CHAPTER 1 — 1
2. CHAPTER 2 — 30
3. CHAPTER 3 — 57
4. CHAPTER 4 — 80
5. CHAPTER 5 — 101
6. CHAPTER 6 — 121
7. CHAPTER 7 — 141
8. CHAPTER 8 — 167
9. CHAPTER 9 — 194
10. CHAPTER 10 — 214
11. EPILOGUE — 235

A Note from Cathy — 241

About Author — 243

Let's Get Social!	244
Also By	245

CHAPTER 1

Kyla Summers was dreaming about silk but working with metal.

After putting the final touches on the timing belt for the 2015 Subaru Forester she'd been struggling with since that morning, she glanced at the clock. Six in the evening. Time to start shutting down. *I'll finish up the head gasket stuff tomorrow*, she thought with a nod. For now, it was time to switch gears. She'd go upstairs from the shop to her apartment. Take a nice hot shower and ensure she got all the grease off before she started working with that new material she'd splurged on.

She was doing a *Game of Thrones* cosplay, and the sky-blue silk was going to be perfect for a new Daenerys dress, she could already tell. She couldn't wait until she could cut into the sumptuous fabric and start piecing it. It was probably silly to start a new outfit only four weeks away from OtakuCon, especially when she had so many partially finished projects that she was going to finish to sell through her friends' booth there, but she wanted to splurge on a fun project.

Her stomach yowled in protest, reminding her that she'd skipped lunch. She might have to wait a little. *Okay, I'll have some dinner first.* She'd just been so damned busy she hadn't had time to eat today.

"Hello?"

She glanced out the open garage door. A man was standing there, in jeans and a flannel shirt, with a hipster beard and a gray cable-knit beanie. He wasn't bad-looking, she thought, but it was almost clinical. It seemed that, like the rest of her body, her hormones were too exhausted to do much lately. "Can I help you?"

"I've been having some trouble with my van," he said. "It's been knocking, and it won't always start."

She frowned. "When you say it won't always start, what does that—"

"Sorry," he interrupted, "but I was hoping I could speak to a mechanic."

She looked pointedly at her gray coveralls. *What do I look like? A waitress?*

But no. She had to be nice to the customer.

"I'm a mechanic," she said, smiling extra-bright. Her friend Hailey called it her Aggressive Friendly posture and was convinced Kyla could maim someone with her smile alone. "And I'm co-owner of this auto shop. I'm happy to help you. Why not start by telling me what the problem is?"

He sneered. He quickly looked a lot less attractive, she thought with an internal shake of the head. Pity. Sexism was never sexy.

"When I try to start it, it makes a noise and now it just won't run."

"What's the make and model?" she asked.

"Um... GMC Van, 1999."

"It's the fuel pump," she said. "Common problem, not too hard to fix. Don't worry."

"You haven't even seen it yet," he whined. Yes, *whined*. "What makes you so sure it's the fuel pump? Isn't that really expensive to fix?"

She kept her smile fixed in place, forcing herself to take deep breaths and go through her response to stressful situations, tensing muscles and relaxing, until she felt the desire to snap at the man fade. "Oh, I have a good guess," she said, making her voice chipper. "We've seen that a lot in GMCs. And it's not that expensive, comparatively speaking." Although she was fully intending to add a slight "asshole tax" if he continued to be so dismissive and petulant.

"I have an art installation I need to set up for this weekend," he said, sounding frantic. "I need the van in the next few days."

She relented a little. She had a soft spot for artists. "That's exciting. What medium?"

He blinked, obviously surprised by her question. "Um... found objects. Mostly collage."

"That's so cool," she said, and he preened at the compliment. "I do fabric arts, myself."

"Oh? Like, tapestries? Or sculpture?"

"Costumes, actually," she said, then saw his puzzled expression. "For comic conventions and things."

He blinked, then laughed. "You mean like that cosplay crap?"

She gritted her teeth, took a deep breath, and did her calming muscle-clench exercises again. "Yes, cosplay," she answered when her voice was sufficiently calm.

He looked around. "Who's the other owner? Where's he?"

"My brother is currently out of town," she said, regretting more than ever that she'd agreed to mind the shop for a long weekend while he went on a ski vacation with his girlfriend, Lindsay. But he was going to propose, and she really liked his girlfriend, Lindsay.

"Your *brother*," he said, with a sage nod, as if everything was now explained. "Huh. When will he be back?"

"Tomorrow." If she smiled any harder, her cheeks would cramp. The fact that Billy was supposed to come home *today* and still hadn't called her didn't help any. She was used to her brother's flakiness, but this was pushing it. *He can work all by* himself *tomorrow,* she thought with ire. With his vacations and all, it felt like she'd been minding the shop more and more lately.

"The problem is, I can't get my van over here," Hipster Beard continued. "I biked over here — you didn't answer your phone, and I left a few messages." He shook his head. "That's not very good business, by the way."

She did the muscle-clench exercise again and gritted her teeth so hard she was surprised they didn't crack.

"I've been busy *working on cars* all day since we're short-handed this week," she said, her voice so chirpy and cheerful she sounded like a Disney princess. "Our message says we get back to customers within twenty-four hours."

He ignored that. "Can you guys send a tow vehicle?"

"We don't tow." She was all about positivity, but her patience had officially run out.

His tone was professorial, and he shook his head. "Again — it's good business to help the customer. Courtesy loaner car and towing are becoming the new norm. I'm in North Bend, and it's really not that far."

Then why don't you pay for it, you idiot?

She sighed. She wanted — very badly — to tell him to take his hipster beard and his stupid van and figure out something else. But the shop always needed business, and besides, she could just dump him on Billy. God knows Billy owed her for this week.

"I'm almost one hundred percent positive it's the fuel pump," she repeated. "Tell you what. You have a piece of firewood?"

His eyes widened. "Um, yeah. Of course I do."

"Of course you do," she repeated with a laugh.

She turned her brightest megawatt smile at him. *I will kill you with my cheer*, she shouted internally.

"Here's what you're going to do. You're going to take a good-sized piece of firewood, stick it under the van, and hit the gas tank."

He took a step away from her. "Are you fucking crazy?"

"Do you want to pay for a tow truck?" she sang at him. "No? Then just smack the gas tank. It'll trip the fuel gauge, and it'll let the car start. Then you drive here, and you park"—she stepped out, pointing to the half-filled parking lot that was kitty-cornered from their small shop—"over there. Okay? Oh, and it'd be best if you had some kind of ride home set up, or Uber or something. We don't offer loaners."

His eyes narrowed. "Smack the gas tank."

She nodded, still beaming like a Girl Scout on speed.

"All right. But if it does any damage, I'm going to expect you to fix it without billing me for it," he said.

She was now grinning hard enough to scare the Joker, she could just feel it. Instead, she said, "Oh, no problem. Chevys are built like tanks, but if you're strong enough to damage the gas tank, then of course I'll cover it."

The guy might have a thick shirt, but she realized on closer inspection that he seemed to be built like a scarecrow — stick arms and all. If he could dent the steel gas tank of a GMC van, she'd eat a carburetor.

"Just smack the gas tank," she repeated. "I'll make sure your van gets taken care of."

He still looked unsure. She sent him a furnace-blast, megawatt smile. He nodded, then walked away toward a restored Schwinn.

She waited until he was out of earshot, then growled, cleaning up the bays and shutting the garage doors. She did a quick glance over the paperwork, sure that nothing was out of place and everything was ready for tackling billing tomorrow — she ought to leave that to Billy, too,

GAME OF HEARTS

she thought. Then she dragged herself upstairs to her apartment.

Billy rented a house a few blocks away, by the river. He lived there with Lindsay. But Kyla was happy to live here in the two-bedroom above the shop. It wasn't much to look at, and sometimes she heard noise from the adjoining business, a local vintner that did its bottling there. Still, it was private, and once the businesses shut down, it was quiet. Also, you couldn't beat the commute.

She locked the door, then stripped, heading toward the shower. She washed off the day, then changed into a pair of yoga pants and a cloud-soft long-sleeved T-shirt. Then she headed into the fridge. She hadn't really had time to grocery shop, either, she thought, looking critically over the contents of her fridge. Some lettuce that had turned brown and slimy — she quickly tossed it. The remnants of a pot roast that hadn't turned out as well as she'd hoped.

She bit her lip, then sighed. "Hell with it," she muttered, dialing Uncle Si's, one of her favorite local restaurants. She ordered her usual, a Mt. Rainier chicken sandwich, complete with caramelized onions and plenty of cheese. She added a salad, in tribute to the wilty mess she'd just tossed out. *At least I'm not getting a pizza*, she reasoned, ignoring the empty pizza box that was mocking her from the recycling bin.

The phone rang at the same time her food was delivered. She juggled the phone as she signed for the meal. "Hello?"

"Kyla?"

"Billy? Where are you? Are you finally home? You said you'd be back yesterday."

"Yeah," he said, "but... some stuff came up."

She shut the front door and put the food down on the battered kitchen table. "How was the trip?"

"Not so good," he said, and she realized he sounded off. His voice was strained.

"Oh, shit," she said, sitting down with a thump. "Lindsay didn't say *no*, did she?"

"What? No. Hell no. She said yes." Now she could hear the smile in his voice, and she heard Lindsay's peal of laughter in the distance.

"Well, that's a relief. Not that I'd blame her. You're a pain in the ass," Kyla teased, but relief washed over her. Billy might be flaky, but he did have a good heart. And he loved Lindsay like crazy. "At least now you're back. We have been busy while you've been gone. I've got a GMC coming in. I'm almost finished with the Subaru, I took care of those two brake jobs and a tune up—"

"All in one long weekend?"

"In four days," she said, rubbing absently at the back of her neck. "Which means, brother dear, that *you* can watch the shop for a few days." She'd sleep in and then start sewing. She started to smile.

"Yeah, about that..." He cleared his throat. "You know how I was going to propose on a mountaintop?"

"Yes," Kyla said, puzzled.

"So, um, the best view was on the top of this Black Diamond slope. So we went up there, and I asked her, and she said yes."

Kyla waited a beat. "So? What's the problem?"

"Still had to make it down the slope," he said, sighing. "And Linds is a *way* better skier than I am."

"You got that right," Lindsay piped up in the background.

"So, um, I was trying to keep up—"

"You were trying to beat me," Lindsay said.

"And, well, this tree came out of nowhere."

Kyla felt her stomach drop again. "Are you all right?"

"What? Well, I'm fine. Sort of."

"Sort of?" Kyla repeated. "What's sort of fine?"

"Um... I broke my arm."

Kyla froze. "You *broke your arm*."

"Yeah. Doc here says I won't be able to work for at least a month..."

All the rest of Billy's words turned into a low buzzing in her ear. She looked over at the second bedroom, her craft room.

"Kyla? You there?"

Kyla sighed. She wouldn't have enough time or energy to finish her dress. Or any of the other costumes she'd promised to her friends to sell. She might not even have time to go to OtakuCon, even if she'd already bought tickets.

But Billy needed her. They'd both taken over the shop from her parents.

She had responsibilities.

"Yeah," she said, slowly. "Yeah, Billy. I'm here."

As always.

Instead of working on costumes, Kyla cleaned up and walked a few blocks down the street to Frost Fandoms, the store where her best friends in the world lived. She hung out with them less since business had picked up, and God knows when things went sideways, you needed your friends. She walked through the front door.

Hailey, looking like a rockabilly goddess in a pair of black capris and a T-shirt with Princess Leia posing as Rosie the Riveter on it, was straightening displays of memorabilia. Cressida, on the other hand, was at the sales counter, poring over the computer, absently twisting her long red hair.

"I need a drink," Kyla said without preamble.

Her friends, sisters Hailey and Cressida Frost, looked at her, then at each other. The third sister, Rachel, was probably at one of her night classes. "Good thing we just closed, then," Cressida said with a gentle smile.

Hailey studied Kyla's face, then nudged her down onto the overstuffed sofa in the main room. "Cadillac margaritas," she pronounced. "This isn't a run-of-the-mill shitty day. Give me a sec, I'll make them."

"What happened?" Cressida asked, her blue eyes full of concern. She sat next to Kyla.

"Billy, that's what," Kyla muttered.

Cressida nodded with sympathy. The Frost sisters had known the Summers family for years, since middle school, and although Cressida rarely saw Billy — her agoraphobia making it nearly impossible for her to leave the house — she still had heard the stories. "What did Billy the Butthead do now?" she asked with a gentle, teasing smile. That had been Kyla's nickname for her older brother for years.

Strangely enough, it was often still accurate.

"You know how he took the long weekend to propose to Lindsay?" Kyla heard the blender whirring and waited until Hailey emerged with a frosty lime beverage. "He broke his arm. Can you believe it?"

Cressida's eyes popped wide open. "What, on purpose?"

"Well, no. Not on purpose," she said, then glowered. "Although I wouldn't put it past him." She took a long, calming, icy sip of the margarita, only wincing slightly at the liberal dose of tequila Hailey had laced it with.

"How long's he down for?" Hailey asked pragmatically.

"A month. At least."

Cressida looked at Hailey woefully. "A whole month? But... but OtakuCon is coming!"

"I *know* this," Kyla moaned. "Believe me. I wanted to do up a new dress, but it looks like I'll just have to finish up Rose Quartz and call it a con. That's if I even have the time to go." She rubbed at her temples.

"*What*?" Hailey roared. "Of course you'll be able to go!"

"You've already bought tickets," Cressida added, looking horrified.

Kyla sighed. Again, stuff she was well aware of. "Hailey, I don't want you and Rachel to think I'm stiffing you on costumes," she reassured her quickly. "I promised that

I'd get you all fitted and get a catalog set up for orders, and we'll still split sales..."

"That is not the point here, and you know it," Hailey said, her normally vibrant voice gentling. "Yeah, the store is still getting its footing, but it's doing much better now that it's shifted from used books to costumes and memorabilia too. Your stuff helps, but the important part here is *you*, not just us. You work your ass off, for the shop and with your costumes."

Kyla squirmed uncomfortably. Compliments, while appreciated, still made her feel weird — she was never quite sure how to play it off casually without sounding like an egotist or an idiot. She shrugged. "Well, I've still got your costume and Rachel's costume pieced and partially constructed. As soon as they're finished, we can take pics, put them on your website and in a brochure/binder thing so people can place orders."

"But Billy's not going to be able to help with the shop at all, right?" Hailey said, eyes narrowing. "When were you planning on doing all this and, I don't know, eating? Or sleeping?"

"You can sleep when you're dead, right?"

Hailey rolled her eyes, getting up. "I'm getting myself a damned margarita," she muttered, stomping to the kitchen.

Cressida sighed. "She's just cranky because Jake is filming in Vancouver," she said with a small smile. Jake, Hailey's TV star boyfriend, had softened a lot of Hailey's rough edges. He treated her like gold, which was good, because Kyla would probably have to kill him if he didn't.

"Still, she's right. You need to take care of yourself, sweetie."

"I am," Kyla said, although her heart wasn't necessarily in it. "I might not be able to go to the con, but there are a ton of conventions in the Pacific Northwest alone all year." She laughed bitterly. "Hopefully Billy will manage to stay healthy so I can actually go to more."

Cressida bit her lip. "Well, I did have news, but I guess this is a bad time to tell you."

"Tell me what?" Kyla's ears perked up. Figuratively speaking, anyway. "Are you guys okay? Having problems with the store? Is Rachel okay? I *knew* she's been working too hard!" Kyla felt her hackles raise. The Frost sisters were family, as far as she was concerned.

"What? No, she's fine, everything's fine. It's just... there's a thing going on, at OtakuCon, that I thought you'd be interested in."

"What thing?"

Cressida popped up, dashing upstairs. Hailey came out, clinking margaritas with Kyla, as they waited for Cressida to return. She came down, her normally pale ivory cheeks pink, her blue eyes twinkling. She handed over a sheaf of papers she'd obviously printed out. "What do you think?"

Puzzled, Kyla looked down, flipping through, scanning the text.

Costumers wanted.

Her pulse picked up. It was a catalog she'd seen before — a branded, well-funded catalog that worked with stuff like Funko and Nerd HQ and even some Marvel stuff. And they were running a contest. Show them what you had, in a variety of categories, and win more than one category in the convention itself, and you could win a big write-up, ten grand — and a photo spread in *Entertainment Weekly*.

Her pulse did more than pick up. It downright sambaed.

"Holy shit," Kyla murmured, envy pulsing through her. "This is amazing."

"You've got so many pieces," Cressida pointed out. "Sure, some of them need work, but you've got willing models, and it's not like you're starting from scratch on all of them. I absolutely know you could win for your work. All you'd need to do is enter them in the OtakuCon costume contest Thursday night, and I'll bet you'd be a lock."

"She's right," Hailey said. "You kick ass."

All modesty aside, Kyla knew her work was above average. In some cases, stellar. She had enough pride in her craftsmanship to know that.

"And I know how badly you've wanted to move your costuming business to the next level."

Kyla could feel her cheeks heat with a blush. Up to this point, she'd only had a few private commissions, and she'd sold through Frost Fandoms' store because she'd argued that she was, essentially, helping out family. But a small part of her wanted something she could call her own. She even had a name and business cards printed up. Summers Child Costumes.

God, she wanted this so badly.

Then she sighed, handing the papers back. "Guess I'll have to hope that they run it again next year," she said, the margarita tasting suddenly acrid. Or was that bitterness all her?

"What?" Hailey said. "Why?" Cressida, on the other hand, just looked mournful.

"I have the shop, remember?" Kyla felt tears start to prick at the corners of her eyes, and she breathed slowly, looking down at her drink until she was sure they weren't going to track down her cheeks. "I don't have the time."

"Remember how Tessa created a video game in just a couple of weeks, to help us promote the store?" Hailey said, getting to her feet. "Remember how we turned this place from a bookstore to what it is now? How we got all those customers? We did that in about a month. You've got this!"

"Yeah, that was when we all pulled together," Kyla pointed out. "Tessa recruited all those coder guys from her company. I helped with costumes. Cress and Rachel helped with orchestrating. Jake and Miles and Simon had star pull — they brought people over from the convention. It took a frickin' village, Hales."

Hailey looked abashed. "There's got to be a way," she muttered stubbornly.

"Yeah, well, unless one of you knows how to sew, or change a timing belt, I don't think that I've got a lot of options."

Hailey frowned.

"No, you really don't know how to fix a timing belt," Kyla said, shaking her head with a rueful grin. "Trust me."

"Does your brother know anyone?" Hailey suggested.

"Why would a stranger help me?"

"Good point," Cressida said hesitantly, then winced, as if hit with some memory. "Maybe you could hire somebody?"

"We do okay, but not hire-another-mechanic okay, not quite," Kyla said. "Otherwise, we'd be turning down more business. Besides that, it's not like there's this huge pool of mechanics I could just pick from. And I wouldn't have time to find and train somebody."

"Damn it," Hailey growled. "There's got to be a way."

Kyla downed the rest of her margarita, thinking of Billy's friends. He did know some mechanics, but nobody she could trust with this. Except...

She blinked.

"Actually," she said, slowly, "I *might* know someone."

"Who?"

"A friend of Billy's. Of the family, really," Kyla hedged. "But I haven't talked to him in years. I'm not even sure where he's living right now. He travels around a lot."

Hailey's eyes narrowed, and Kyla felt a blush creep up her cheeks. "Who is it?" Hailey repeated.

Kyla sighed. "Um... Jericho Salomon."

Now Hailey's carefully drawn eyebrows jumped to her hairline. "The *hottie*?"

Kyla shrugged. Hailey wasn't wrong. "Yeah."

"He used to work in your shop, right? Basically lived at your house," Hailey mused. "What's he doing now? Do you know?"

"Traveling around, like I said. Works at various shops as a mechanic, does custom work on bikes and cars."

"So why wouldn't he work at Summers Auto?" Hailey said.

Kyla swallowed hard. "He left Snoqualmie because of some shit with his family," she said. "He hasn't been back in a while."

Nine years, to be exact.

Hailey brushed the statement away. "He's a grown-ass man. He can deal with a little static. And besides, you need the help. Billy broke his arm."

"He might say no." Now Kyla was feeling her pulse pick up hectically.

"If you don't ask, it's a guaranteed hard no, isn't it?"

Kyla cursed herself. "I'll, um, text tonight. I guess." Then she took a big, cooling sip of her margarita. She was going to need all the liquid courage she could get her hands on if she was going to call the love of her life — or at least, the crush of her adolescent dreams — and ask him to help out in her shop for the next few weeks.

It took Jericho Salomon half an hour to get from his bike to the back room of the Rusty Wrench, a biker bar about an hour outside of Vegas. When he'd first joined the Machinists, a gearhead biker club, back when he was seventeen years old and freshly dropped out of high school, the club meetings took place whenever the group was close enough, organized on their rinky-dink website that somebody's nephew had set up. Back then, they were about twenty guys, max. Usually only ten or so together at any particular time.

Now, there were easily fifty people here in Vegas alone. He shook his head. And this was just a *monthly regional* meeting. It was kind of nuts, the way the group had grown — word spreading through bulletin boards and social media and shit. It was as if the Machinists somehow had become *fashionable*. Jericho blamed that on the all those reality TV shows about custom builders and riding. People were learning the joy of building with their hands and creating a machine that could have you roaring across the open countryside, wind in your hair and freedom in your heart. Which was part of why he loved motorcycles, riding, building and the club.

Mike Branch waved at him from across the crowded bar, and he nodded in response, slowly winding his way through the packed house. Mike ushered him to the private room upstairs, where it was thankfully quieter, with a table where they usually played poker, a small freestanding bar, and a bunch of chairs.

Mike Branch was a six-two black man, corded with muscle, around fifty years old or so. He was one of the founders of the Machinists, the one who had suggested the name, who had printed up T-shirts as a joke back in the day. He didn't ride as much as the others since he had settled down in Vegas and started a family. Now, he owned an awesome shop where a lot of the Machinists had work done. He did fucking phenomenal custom work

— not necessarily the flashy paint jobs and chrome with flames bullshit you saw on the reality shows, although they could do that if customers wanted. Mostly, they made bikes the way old clockmakers made clocks — things of beauty on the inside, as well as on the outside, if you knew what you were looking for.

Mike had given Jericho a couch to sleep on and a job when he'd first left Washington State, all pissy and determined... and, if he was honest, scared. Mike was a guy he looked up to.

"What took you so long?" This from Pedro Gonzalez, the other leader of the Machinists. He was the one who had met Jericho outside a different biker bar, in Seattle. Jericho had only been seventeen, so he hadn't even been allowed in the place, but he'd hung out in the parking lot, bumming cigarettes off of older guys and talking about motorcycles. When Pedro had a weird difficulty and his bike had gotten fucked up, Jericho had helped him fix it. From there, he'd told Pedro about getting kicked out by his mom. Pedro had connected him with Mike. By the time he was eighteen, he'd been a full-fledged member of the Machinists.

Not that they were a biker club the way TV portrayed them — they didn't have patches, didn't wear colors. They weren't like the Hell's Angels or Bandidos or Outlaws. No, the Machinists were just a bunch of gearheads.

They were Jericho's kind of people.

"It took me all this time just to make it through that crowd," Jericho said, pulling out a chair, turning it and straddling it. At six foot seven, it was hard for him to find furniture he could comfortably fit in. "Are they all Machinists now?"

"If they aren't, they want to be," Pedro said, shaking his head.

"My son says that we've gotten more new sign ups on the website in the past three weeks," Mike added. "They're from all over. We've got over a hundred people signed up, saying they're gonna go to the Rally in Idaho, and more are planning on showing up if they can."

"What the hell do they want?" Pedro said, sounding surly. "They're acting like this is some kinda AMA club. Asking about dues, voting, shit like that. This thing is getting kind of out of hand."

"That's because we're the shit," a new voice chimed in, entering the room. "And with this many people, we're ready for something big."

Jericho looked over at the new participant. Trevor was in his late twenties, maybe early thirties, and looked more like a "typical" biker — leather jacket, jeans, bandana over dirty-blond hair and a scruffy beard. He'd made a name for himself in the Machinists by winning a competition for a bike build in Vegas.

Privately, Jericho didn't think that Trevor had done most of the work for that prize-winning build, and he was fairly certain that at least half the bike parts were stolen. But the code of the Machinists was simple: live and let live, don't get in other people's business. Hell, when Jericho's Mom had kicked him out, Pedro hadn't asked why, and nobody else had grilled him, ever. They'd given him chances and choices, which was just what he needed at the time. He might not agree with or like Trevor, particularly, but he wasn't going to go throwing judgment around like a hypocrite.

"What do you mean by something big?" Pedro asked, his voice ripe with suspicion. "I didn't want the club to be as big as it is *now*, for Chrissake. It looks like hipster happy hour down there, and I don't think a bunch of those guys know a two-stroke from a four-stroke."

Mike chuckled. "They want to learn," he said. "You weren't born knowing every damned thing about an engine, either. Only guy who might've been born knowing all there is to know about bikes is Jericho here."

Jericho suppressed a small smile, shrugging.

"Yeah, he's got the gift," Pedro admitted. "Seventeen-year-old punk kid, telling me why my bike was broken. Had some balls on you back then. And a smartass mouth."

"Still pretty mouthy," Mike pointed out with a grin.

"Hey, I got better," Jericho countered, grinning back. "Back then, I was just a dumb kid trying to make an impression."

"And now?" Mike asked, eyes twinkling.

"Still dumb," he admitted ruefully, "but at least I don't have so much to prove."

They all laughed except Trevor, who looked impatient. "Pedro's right. A lot of these new guys just think that we're gonna let 'em in and teach them everything."

"Why wouldn't we?" Mike asked. "I don't mind teaching."

"You mind losing money taking out all the time to teach dumb shits who don't know their ass from their elbow?" Pedro asked. "Because for a guy who's building his business, you gotta admit that's pretty dumb."

Mike shot Pedro some side-eye. "Please tell me Mr. Hand-to-mouth ain't telling me how to run my successful business."

"I'm just saying we're getting too big," Pedro complained. "It's just a big fucking mess."

"Exactly," Trevor leaped in. "What we need to do is set up, like, membership levels. And you gotta earn your way if you want to get higher. Show that you know your stuff, that you're loyal to the club."

"That could work," Pedro said, rubbing the scruff on his chin.

"I'm not loving the 'loyal to the club' stuff," Mike added, looking concerned.

"Well, it's a lot of work organizing this shit, right? The meet-ups, the whole thing," Trevor continued, his eyes bright. "We could just have them help out. There's always little stupid stuff on a build. You could have them, like, clean out your garage. Do other, you know, piddly shit that's annoying."

Now Mike smiled slowly. "I do hate taking the oil to recycling."

"Exactly. This way, you get help for free, they get to earn their way to higher levels. Like, what you call 'em. Fraternity pledges."

Pedro rolled his eyes. "Because I been in a fraternity, dawg. Obviously."

Mike shook his head. "We gonna make 'em learn a step dance, too?"

"We could make 'em do anything we want," Trevor said, his grin broad. "Run errands. Go across the damned state to pick up parts. Whatever. We. Want."

"Hazing. Initiation. Hierarchy. Like a gang," Jericho said quietly. "Or like the big motorcycle clubs. Hell's Angels. Bandidos. The ones that got killed down in Texas — the ones on FBI watch lists. That what you want, Trev?"

The laughter fell off. Trevor looked irritated, while Pedro and Mike suddenly looked thoughtful.

"I am *not* into that one-percenter bullshit," Mike said decisively. "Drugs and crime and all that. I run a clean shop. I don't get mixed up in that shit, and y'all know it."

"I'm a little more tolerant," Pedro said, then held up his hands defensively when Mike glared at him. "I mean, no, we're not gonna be running around murdering people or fighting other clubs. But some of the guys do, um, 'odd jobs' to stay on their wheels and keep riding. They don't exactly have a huge array of legit job opportunities. If they keep their shit together and stay off cops' radar, I don't particularly care."

Trevor nodded at that. "That's what I'm talking about. We're just teaching loyalty," he said. "Loyalty to the club and each other. If you get in trouble, we've got your back."

Jericho gritted his teeth. Trevor's idea of trouble tended to be criminal — either a member getting mixed up in shit he shouldn't or getting caught by the cops and needing bail money.

"If we're going that route... No. You know what? *No.* We're not fucking going that route," Mike said sharply.

"I think that there's room for discussion," Trevor said, his voice low and deceptively mild. "I think that the people out there might have other ideas. I've been listening to them. I'm just saying... you don't give 'em some direction, god knows where they'd wind up, right? We'd be better than that shit."

Mike looked troubled. They were bringing on a lot of young guys lately. "They're grown men," he said, but sounded nervous.

Jericho shifted uneasily. He hadn't been grown when he hooked up with the Machinists. He knew, daily, that he was lucky he hadn't fallen in with a worse crowd.

"What do you think, J?" Pedro asked. Pedro always valued his opinion, and Jericho realized that he really had come a long way. He'd been one of the stupid young club members nine years ago. Now, the guys who started the club were asking his opinion. He weighed the responsibility heavily, wondering how to respond.

Suddenly, his phone rang.

He blinked, surprised. He rarely gave out his phone number. Basically, the only people who had it were sitting in this room with him. Who the hell was calling him?

"You got a girlfriend, finally, kemosabe?" Pedro said, laughing.

Jericho absently flipped him off. "Pendejo," he said, making Pedro laugh harder. He glanced at the screen.

The name read: Kyla.

He half smiled even as he felt a bubble of confusion. Kyla was the kid sister of his best friend — hell, practically one of his best friends — in junior high and high school. He'd slept on their family couch more times than he attended school junior year. She would email him sometimes, jokes and stuff. And she always, always texted him on his birthday.

It was kinda nice, actually. She was the only one who remembered.

He glanced at the clock readout. Eleven o'clock.

Why the hell was Kyla *calling* him, instead of texting or emailing?

Something's wrong.

He was out of the chair before it rang again. "Sorry, I gotta get this," he blurted out to the guys, hitting accept even as he was heading to the balcony and into the cooling night, ignoring the sounds of the crowd below.

"Ky? What's up? You okay?"

"Um... hi, Jericho." Kyla sounded a little slurred.

The fuck? Was Kyla even old enough to drink? Then he remembered — it'd been years since she'd been a teen. Still, she sounded upset. "Babe, what's wrong?"

"Billy broke his arm."

Jericho tensed. Jesus. There was no telling what could happen at an auto shop. Could've gotten it caught under an engine block or something — multiple fracture, nasty healing. "What happened? Did it happen at the shop? Is he all right?"

"No, it's fine," Kyla reassured him. "He hit a tree."

Jericho blinked. "Sorry, what? It sounded like you said he... hit a *tree*?"

"Yeah."

He let out a surprised laugh. "How the hell did he do that?"

"He was skiing... It's a long story," Kyla said with a little tremulous giggle. "Anyway, he's going to be down for a month."

Jericho let out a slow whistle. "That sucks," he said, still puzzled. Why had she called with this, rather than text or email? And why did she sound so nervous?

"My parents are RVing right now. They're in New England, and I think this month they're planning on hitting Canada or something," she continued. "It's really important to them, and I don't want to worry them, and I'd hate to interrupt their trip because it means so much to them now that Dad's retired and all..."

"Okay..." He frowned, still baffled.

"So, I'm, um, by myself this month. At the shop. But the thing is, I, um, have this, ah, project that I promised I'd do. Well, that I *want* to do," she said, and he could practically hear her blush over the phone. She took in a deep breath. "And we're really backed up at the shop. And, um, I could, uh..."

"Babe," he said slowly, "do you need some help at the shop?"

"*Yes!*" She let out an explosive sigh. "I don't... I mean, I'm sure you're probably busy," she said, words tumbling over each other like circus clowns exiting a car. "Or you're traveling, right? Because you're usually busy and traveling. Oh, God, forget I called!"

He couldn't help himself — he laughed. "Ky, slow down. Breathe, will you? It's fine."

"It's just, I could really use some help. If you've got time. Maybe... the next week or so?"

He felt the smile latch onto his face. Kyla was ridiculously cute. She was also ridiculously self-sufficient. Ever since she was a kid, he'd known — she was the one who provided the help and care. Not the one who asked for it.

If she was asking for help, she must really be in a jam.

"But if you can't, that's fine. Really. Completely, totally fine," she continued to babble. "I mean, I totally, completely, absolutely understand..."

"Shut up and let me say yes, okay?" he said with a chuckle.

She paused, then let out a little squeak of delight. "Really?"

"It'll take me a day or two to get there, but I'll help out. Okay?"

"Oh, thank you! You are awesome. Like, epic hero awesome. They will write songs about you. People will wave banners and chant 'dilly, dilly' and bake you cakes..." She was trailing off as whatever she'd been drinking kicked into overdrive.

"See you, kiddo." He hung up. Then he headed back in. Mike and Trevor were arguing, while Pedro looked at Jericho, concerned.

"Everything cool?" Pedro asked.

"Yeah," Jericho said. "Family stuff."

Pedro's eyebrows jumped up. "For real? Thought you hadn't talked to that bitch since she kicked your ass out."

Jericho winced. Before he could say anything, Mike reached over, slapping Pedro on the back of the head.

"What the fuck?" Pedro yelped, glaring at him.

"You don't call a guy's momma a bitch," Mike said sharply.

"It wasn't my mom," Jericho said quickly. He had thought of his mother, but he quashed it, as always. "This is... well, my best friend's family. They were basically my family back in the day. They have an auto shop. He got hurt, they're shorthanded and in serious trouble, and they need my help."

"In that little town you're from?" Pedro asked. "Snow-tummy? Snowwhatta? Snowwackachackalatte?"

"Snoqualmie," Jericho said with no humor. Pedro had always teased him about the name when they'd first met. But he hadn't talked about, or tried to think about, Snoqualmie in nine years now.

The thought struck him. *Now, you've just agreed to go back.*

Another flash of his mother: her angry face, their ugly words.

"And you're just going?" Trevor interrupted his memory, sounding pissed. "But we've got big stuff to nail down, dude! This shit is important!"

"It can wait until the yearly meeting," Jericho said. "That's only a month away. Probably the best time to make a big decision that affects the whole club."

"I don't know how much discussion we'll need," Mike said. "At least, not about the one-percenter-styled stuff. But the club's getting big enough that we have to make some choices."

"You know I'm there," Pedro said, rubbing his hands together. "Rally, baby! Idaho!"

"How long you gonna be gone?" Trevor pressed.

Jericho looked back at him, his tone cool. "Probably just a week or so," he said. "Maybe longer."

"Well, do what you gotta, and then get your ass back here," Mike said. "You're like the right-hand man of the club, and we need you, too. We're family."

Jericho sighed. He was right on that front. The Machinists had been there for him, giving him a life, a place to belong.

"I'll be back as soon as I can," he said, and meant it.

CHAPTER 2

Two days later, Kyla was still mortified. She'd had one too many liquid courage and consolation margaritas with Hailey — Cressida didn't partake — and by the time she'd ambled back to her apartment, she'd been a blithering idiot. The call with Jericho had felt like a dream. When she'd woken up hungover and checked her call record to see if she'd actually gone through with it, it felt more like a nightmare.

Now, she felt like a whiny loser for reaching out. Sure, it'd be great to get the costumes done. But to ask for help? She'd handled the shop by herself plenty of times over the past few years since her father had retired, hadn't she? And besides, it wasn't like she was planning on quitting the shop just to start her costume business, right?

Her heart gave a wistful pang at the thought, surprising her. She shook it off. Nobody she knew who cosplayed made a full-time living making costumes. It just wasn't reasonable.

Kyla was nothing if not reasonable.

She checked the computer with her work docket. "Billy, don't take on any new customers, okay? We're backlogged as it is."

"Like I could figure out this software," Billy protested from the front office. "There's a reason I usually work in the bays and not here in the hotbox."

He called the office the hotbox because it didn't have air conditioning. She hid her growl of irritation underneath the sound of the lift. She resented that Billy shirked the administrative duties, too, leaving a lot of the promotion and billing on her. He was a kick-ass mechanic, which made up for some of it, but then, so was she, and she'd still managed to figure out the damned software.

She worked all morning, knocking out a brake job and diagnosing a faulty muffler. Van Guy had finally done what she'd told him — the smack test — and driven his vehicle over. If she worked late, she'd probably be able to stay ahead.

But what about the costume contest?

She gritted her teeth. If she wasn't too worn out — and that was a big if — she'd finish up her Princess Quartz outfit.

She heard Billy talking and suddenly realized he must be on the phone. Since Lindsay was at work — she was a pediatric nurse — and Billy never talked on the phone to anybody, she realized he must be dealing with a customer. They'd been tight the first few years when they'd taken over from their dad, especially when she'd insisted on renovations. She knew his instinct was always to take all the customers they could handle. And then add a few more.

There was a lull, and she strode through the open bays and down the small hallway to the office. "You on the phone?" she called.

"No."

She gritted her teeth, storming in. "Billy, dammit, please tell me you didn't take on any new customers," she said from the doorway. "I'm slammed enough as it is."

"No problem! As it happens, I've got the answer to all your problems right here," he said with his usual broad grin.

She wanted to strangle him. "Unless you've magically produced a mechanic from out of your butt, I sincerely doubt that."

Billy burst out laughing, and she heard a low responding chuckle. Surprised, she stepped farther into the office. She hadn't realized there was anyone else there.

Oh, God. Don't be a customer.

She stepped past the high filing cabinet just as the other person stood up — and kept standing up, or so it seemed. The man unfolded himself from the rickety office chair, and he looked almost seven feet tall.

She goggled. She couldn't help it. Jet-black hair, wavy, curling at the ends of his collar and brushing his shoulders. Which, by the way, were incredible. Holy hell, broad shoulders. The guy was yoked. He was wearing a black T-shirt that said Machinists with a skull-and-crossbones, where the crossbones were wrenches. It stretched over a chest that looked carved out of marble. He was also wearing riding leathers.

Holy shit. Her mouth went dry as the Sahara out of sheer, unrelenting *thirst*.

Her eyes roamed some more. She needed to stop staring at the guy's bod, she realized. She was objectifying. She was embarrassing herself. There was an off chance she might be struck blind by his brutal sexiness.

She slid her gaze back up, over what she figured was a washboard-flat six-pack, and past tanned, muscular forearms. Up to his face. Dark eyes, a brown so deep it was almost black. High, chiseled cheekbones. And a smile that...

Wait a minute.

Her jaw dropped. "Jericho? Is that you?"

His smile widened.

"In the flesh, baby."

She stared for just a second longer.

Then, like a bullet out of a gun, she launched herself at him.

· ♥ · ♥ · ♥ · ♥ · ♥ ·

Jericho burst out laughing as Kyla sprung on him, throwing her arms around his neck. Reflexively, he bent down and lifted her from the waist until her feet dangled from the floor.

"Oh, my God!" she cried, squeezing him hard. He squeezed her back, feeling his heart clench a little. She wriggled until he put her down. "You're here. You're actually here!"

"You guys are family. Of course I came," he replied, kissing her cheek and putting her back on her feet. He took in her appearance. She was wearing gray coveralls that masked her shape, although in deference to the heat, they were unzipped quite a bit. As he'd hugged her, he couldn't help but notice that she didn't *feel* quite the same as she had before, either. Of course, when he'd left, she'd been fifteen or sixteen, and her curves hadn't been quite this ample.

Or pronounced, he realized. Then immediately felt like a creep for realizing. He swallowed hard.

"Damn, Ky," he said, his voice sounding raspy to his own ears. "You went and grew up on me."

"Nine. *Nine* years you've been gone. What were you expecting?" she said, playfully punching his arm. "You grew up, too. Or at least grew out."

He barked out a laugh, then another louder one when she blushed.

"I mean, look at you." She rubbed her hand over his shoulders. "What, did you discover steroids? Are you an MMA fighter or something?"

"You don't like it?" Just to mess with her, he flexed his pecs, enjoying the way her eyes popped at the motion.

"Holy cannoli," she chirped, then grinned. "I think I just got wet!"

"Oh, gross," Billy groaned, rubbing his good hand over his face. "New rule: if Jericho's going to work here, you guys can't do that shit again."

"Do what?" Jericho exchanged a grin and wink with Kyla.

They'd started over-the-top fake flirting to drive Billy up a wall when she turned fifteen, after Billy had tried to throw his weight and tell Kyla that she could essentially *never* have sex, and then told Jericho that he'd "better not get any ideas." It was like waving red in front of a pair of bulls. They'd mocked Billy mercilessly ever since. Despite that, Jericho hadn't thought of her that way, or had tried not to. The truth was, with Billy's football and baseball practices, Jericho had hung out with Kyla as much as his best friend. In a lot of ways, she was just as good a friend. He valued that friendship.

That said, messing with Billy was one of his favorite hobbies, and hearing the squeaky-clean and super-cheerful Kyla try to talk dirty was consistently hilarious.

He leaned back, pretending to preen. "What can I say? Your sister can't keep her hands off me."

She smirked, batting her eyes at him and blowing him a kiss.

"Tease," he growled. She burst into giggles.

Billy rubbed his temple. "You guys are going to give me an aneurysm."

She leaned against Jericho, and he caught her scent — like lemon and axle grease. It was a surprisingly pleasant combination. He felt a bubble of happiness.

He'd been tense since he crossed the city line into Snoqualmie. Just being back here, where he'd spent the better part of his childhood, had been anxiety inducing. He'd even felt it when he was here talking with Billy. He'd hung out with Billy a few times since he'd left — they'd gone on a fishing trip in Alaska, and they'd had a few wild weekends in Vegas with some of the Machinists. But Jericho hadn't set foot in Snoqualmie in nine years and would've continued to avoid it if the Summers weren't having such a bad time. If Kyla hadn't called.

"So, you're going to help out?" Kyla interrupted his thoughts. Her gentle moss-green eyes were hopeful. "I mean, it's not too much of an inconvenience? You had to have other stuff going on."

"Nothing I couldn't handle."

He saw her throat work as she swallowed, and her eyes went glassy. She closed them, then took a deep breath. "I'm not going to lie. It's going to be a huge difference to have you here. But I don't want to take you away from—"

"You're not taking me away from anything," he interrupted before she could work herself up. "I am right where I want to be, sunshine. Okay?"

She looked askance at him.

"Do you really think anybody can make me do something I don't want to do?" he asked with a note of humor.

Billy chuckled. "I'd like to see them try."

Kyla finally relented, her smile warming up until it was incandescent. "It's really, really good to have you here," she said, putting a hand on his arm, then hugging him again, snuggling against his chest.

Instinctively, he curved his arm around her, pulling her flush against him, and then he felt his body tighten in response. Which surprised him enough to have him choke a little.

"You okay?" she asked, pulling away.

"Fine," he croaked, putting some space between them and getting a paper cup of water from the water dispenser they had for customers. "So. What are we looking at? What do you need done?"

Billy and Kyla exchanged glances. Kyla leaned against a wall, crossing her arms — which made her cleavage plump up, he couldn't help but notice. He really had to stop noticing that kind of shit, he thought, slightly disturbed. Instead, he focused on Billy's serious expression.

"Well, I can't work for a while," Billy said. "Doctor will say exactly when after they finish reading the X-rays and get results back from the tests and stuff. But I'm out of commission when it comes to repair work."

"But you're more than able to type one-handed," Kyla said with a note of warning in her voice. Billy sighed in response.

"You're better at it than I am, though."

She sighed. Billy scowled.

"Maybe I can help," Jericho said, and they stared at him for a moment. "Hey. I'm not just a pretty face."

"You're also a smokin' hot bod," Kyla quipped, laughing.

Billy rolled his eyes. "God help me."

Jericho chuckled. "I love it when you objectify me, sweetheart," he said dryly. "But seriously. I've been working at a bunch of different shops. There's some great software out there to help with, like, estimates and billing. I can put in a few calls. I'm sure some friends could make some suggestions."

Kyla looked impressed, which made his chest puff out a little, even though it was probably a stupid thing to be proud of. He hadn't cared about not going to college or anything, and he'd spent the past nine years loving the fact that he had nothing to prove to anyone. But sometimes, like when he was working on a custom job for some rich asshole, he'd feel their judgment on him like a suffocating blanket.

The Summers had never looked at him like that, not ever. They'd always believed in him. But her admiration was still nice.

Billy, on the other hand, was looking at him like he walked on water. "If you can make billing easier, I will buy you your own body weight in beer."

"What I really was looking for was sexual favors," Jericho said. "But I was expecting Kyla to provide those. No offense."

"Oh, that is a given," Kyla said breezily, winking at him. "Even if you couldn't fix a lawnmower."

"As it happens, I'm pretty handy with all sorts of tools," he said, watching Billy's frustration grow. "I'm good at drilling *and* nailing."

"Man, I am gonna hit that like a hydraulic press," she fake purred.

Jericho smirked, even as he discovered his body was continuing to act on his ridiculous jokes. *Really? Is this happening? Should we get ready to roll?*

"Would you *stop* it?" Billy groaned. "Seriously. How could I have forgotten what you two are like? You're just lucky I know you're kidding."

Jericho shifted his weight, focusing hard on the biggest turnoffs he could think of: the ugliest custom job he'd ever seen — all tacky chrome, multicolor neon flames, skulls, plastic, fake-boobed women and Grateful Dead bears. He was grateful that his denim was loose enough to hide the thickness that was starting to develop down below.

He'd *always* kidded with Kyla. But now, even with his best friend and her big brother *right there*, the flirting felt a little less like kidding and more like...

Foreplay.

He winced. "So, I've got my bag and shit," Jericho said. "I'm happy to see what kind of stuff you've got lined up for the week. Then I guess I'll follow you to your house, huh?"

Billy blinked. "My house?"

Kyla hadn't really talked about where he'd be sleeping, so Jericho had just assumed. Now, he felt a little odd. "Um, where I'll be crashing while I work here?"

Billy looked uncomfortable. "Sorry, dude, I wasn't thinking. I, um, live with Lindsay. We bought a one-bedroom house, down by the river."

"Oh." He was continually surprised at the almost dreamy look Billy got when he talked about his girlfriend.

It was nice. Made Jericho a little envious, in fact. "I can just crash on the couch. Hell, I lived on your couch for years."

"You weren't quite so big then," Billy pointed out.

"I *know*, right?" Kyla added, her voice ripe with innuendo, then let out a peal of laughter. Jericho let out a surprised shout.

"Seriously, Ky. Knock it off," Billy said with absent irritation.

"Don't worry," Kyla said. "I asked him for help. He can stay here."

Jericho raised an eyebrow. "You mean, bunk on the floor here in the office?" He grimaced. He wanted to help, but camping out on the floor of the cramped little office probably wasn't ideal. "It's fine, I can just get a motel room."

"Wait," Billy interrupted, frowning. "Ky, you asked Jericho here? It's not just a visit?"

Jericho rolled his eyes. "When was the last time I visited?"

"Not here in the office," Kyla quickly cut in. "And no, I don't want you spending any extra money on a motel room. You can stay with me. Upstairs."

Jericho's eyes widened in confusion. "Huh?" he squeaked.

Kyla sighed. "We own the building," she said, surprising him. "Mom's idea. We rent the space next door to a local vintner — they bottle their wine and store it over there. But there's a two-bedroom apartment above the garage. That's where I live."

"Oh. Okay," Jericho said, temporarily thrown. It shouldn't— Hell, he'd slept on the floor or couch at the Summers' house almost every day of his sophomore year in high school, and he and Kyla had crashed on an air mattress watching scary movies when Billy was off at prom. But now, it just felt a little... weird. He wasn't quite sure why.

"Is that okay?" she asked, fidgeting a little. "You know?"

"What, us..." He stopped himself before he could say *sleeping together*. What the hell? Where had that come from? This was Kyla. "Sharing a place?"

What the hell are you going on about? his subconscious poked at him. *What is wrong with you?*

He closed his eyes. He was more tired from the long ride than he'd thought.

"I don't see there being any problems with it. Unless... your boyfriend's gonna mind?" Jericho made his voice as jokey as possible. "I mean, I am pretty intimidating."

Billy snickered before she had a chance to respond. "Kyla doesn't have a boyfriend. Not since that loser who broke up with her before we inherited the shop." Kyla glared at him, and Billy looked immediately apologetic. "You've got to admit it. He *was* a loser."

"There's plenty of room, and I'd love to have you stay," she said, still glaring at Billy. "Besides, I've got a California king and a mattress that can take a pounding, if you know what I mean."

"And a daybed in that tiny spare room," Billy added, ignoring her.

"Thanks," Jericho said to Kyla. "I'll take it."

Kyla huffed. "All right, you two, that van isn't going to fix itself, and I still need to replace the head gasket on that Forester. I'm gonna get on it. You know where the coveralls are and everything." She walked past Billy, rolling her eyes at him. He pretended to glower at her. Then she looked over her shoulder at Jericho, her eyes soft and glowing. "And Jericho?"

"Yeah?"

Her full lower lip curved into a smile. "Thanks."

He watched her disappear out the door, then turned back to Billy, who was still frowning.

Get your head together, Jericho. He shook the cobwebs out. "God, you two working together," Jericho said to Billy finally. "I'm surprised she hasn't killed you."

"She's been tempted, but I'm a hell of a mechanic," Billy said. "And she's better with business than I am, so I don't bug her too much." He was still frowning, though.

Now Jericho felt uncomfortable. "You know she and I are just kidding around, right?" he said, suddenly concerned. "I'd never—"

"Oh, I know," Billy said, waving his arm with the cast, then wincing. "No, I'm not bothered by that. I know you're just kidding. You two have always been friends, and really, you're like family. Besides, she's not your type."

Jericho tilted his head. "Huh?"

"She's... you know."

"No, I don't," Jericho said, confused.

Billy sighed, looked at the door, then lowered his voice. "She's kinda... heavy."

Jericho felt anger for a second. He loved the guy like a brother, but Billy really could be an asshole. Kyla might not be a stick figure, and yeah, she had more padding than a lot of the girls he'd seen hanging out at various Machinist gatherings and biker bars. Honestly, she was larger than a lot of the women he'd dated. But he also knew her, and cared about her, more than almost any woman he knew.

He frowned. Beyond that, she also had a face like a frickin' angel, and that smile was blinding. She was also sweet, selfless, and thoughtful. Combine that with her devilish sense of humor, and any guy would be lucky to have her.

He thought quickly back to their hug. She also had crazy-soft skin, he remembered. And her curves had felt damned good when pressed against him.

Of course, saying that to her brother was probably not the best idea, either.

"Billy, don't be a dick," he said instead.

Billy grinned weakly. "See?" he said. "You protect her, just like a big brother. She's like family."

Jericho didn't answer, because right now, the last thing he was feeling was brotherly.

· ♥ · ♥ · ♥ · ♥ · ♥ ·

Kyla was pleasantly surprised at how well the rest of the day went. Jericho rolled up his proverbial sleeves and dove right in, looking over the punch list of repairs and working on the van's fuel gauge, which Van Guy would probably be thrilled with — he'd wanted a man to work on his van, and you couldn't get more stereotypically manly than Jericho Salomon.

Lindsay brought by pizzas for dinner, and they all caught up, even though Kyla kept sneaking peeks at her phone. It was almost nine o'clock, and she still had a lot to do. She needed to start sewing the Megara costume, and she was using two different shades of chiffon, which was a slippery bitch to work with. Jericho and Billy were having a great time catching up, and honestly, so was she. Besides that, Billy didn't know how much she was doing with the cosplay. Not that his opinion mattered, but if he poked fun at her now, when she was tired, stressed, and overextended, she had the tendency to... well, bite his head off. And she didn't feel like getting into a kick-down drag-out in front of Lindsay and Jericho.

She saw Billy wince, rubbing his shoulder, and Lindsay frowned. "All right, cowboy, time to get you to bed," she said, urging him up. "I'll drop him off tomorrow morning — if he's feeling up to it."

"I'm fine," Billy grumbled, but Kyla could see the look of affection mixed in with the grumpiness. Lindsay was really his perfect match. "See you in the morning."

She waved good-bye to them, then lowered the doors on the bays and locked up. Jericho followed her with his bag as they walked up the stairs to her apartment.

As she let him in, she took in the place, a little aghast, wishing she'd taken the time to clean. She'd just been really busy with the costumes, and it had taken up all of her time. She could only imagine how he saw it. There was an okay-sized living room, although it now seemed tiny with him towering in it. There was a beat-up chocolate-brown leather couch, an overstuffed microfiber recliner, and a fireplace. She quickly picked up some takeout wrappers, tossing them, then cleaned up her cereal bowl from breakfast and a collection of water glasses from various tables, putting them all in the dishwasher.

"This your parents' kitchen table?" he asked as she tidied, rubbing his hand over the maple surface.

"Yeah. When they sold the house and got the RV, they told us to take what we wanted. Some stuff is in storage, in case they want to settle down again, but I grabbed the table and chairs."

"Looks good in here," he said. "Cozy."

"Thanks. I wanted it to be kind of like a hobbit hole."

He raised an eyebrow. "You're still into all that, huh?"

"Oh, you have no idea," she muttered as she loaded the dishwasher and got it running. "Sorry. It's not usually this messy. I've just been really busy."

"I'll bet," he said, opening a cabinet and grabbing a glass. He poured himself a glass of water, and it warmed her to see him making himself at home. "Seems like Billy's been out of commission for a while, with vacation and now the injury. You've been really working, huh?"

It was nice of him to notice. "Yeah. And I've, um, got some personal stuff I'm doing, too." She sighed. Best to just get it out of the way. "Listen, I think you should sleep in my bedroom."

She glanced over to see him, staring at her with wide eyes, the glass paused halfway to his mouth. *"Pardon?"*

"I'll be in the spare room," she said with a snicker, feeling only a little insulted. "Don't worry. Your virtue is still safe."

He burst out with surprised laughter, but she swore he was blushing a little. Seeing this seven-foot-tall hottie looking like a shy virgin was, frankly, hilarious.

She shook her head. "You're not going to fit on my daybed, in the first place. And in the second place... well, you can't be in the spare room. I have, well, stuff going on in there."

Now he looked curious. "Like what? A meth lab?" He shot her a look of mock seriousness. "You breakin' bad, Kyla Summers?"

"Well, it's not like I have a basement," she pointed out, which got him laughing again. She'd missed this — joking with him. He was a fun guy, and they'd always made each other laugh, even when they were having shitty days. "No, no. It's just... listen, do you know what cosplay is?"

"Not really."

"It's costumes. Elaborate ones, for, like, comic conventions and stuff," she explained. "I like making costumes."

She waited, bracing herself for ridicule, like the asshat artist van owner. Instead, he nodded. "Okay. I see that. You were always good at making clothes. And you were always into that fantasy stuff — *Lord of the Rings* and Narnia or whatever." He paused. "Can I see some of it?"

She started, surprised. "Really? You want to see the costumes?"

"Sure. Why not?"

"It's kind of chaos right now," she said, opening the door and turning on the light.

Chaos didn't even begin to cover it. She had two adjustable dress forms. One she'd draped with muslin, approximating the Daeneyrs dress. The other she'd pinned with the pieces of the Liliana dress, ensuring it'd fit Rachel. The Megara dress was carefully laid out across her sewing table, ready for assembly. There were also a number of props she'd painted that were drying on the small table she'd jammed in there, as well as sketches and inspiration pictures she'd stuck to the enormous corkboard she had covering one wall. The closet was filled to the gills with fabric, details, old costumes, and various accoutrements.

He let out a low whistle. "This is…"

"Insane?" She let out a nervous laugh. "Yeah, I guess."

"This is amazing," he said instead. "You're really into this stuff, huh?"

She nodded. "Remember the Frost sisters?" When he nodded, she said, "They still live in that three-story over on Railroad. They turned the lowest level into a bookstore and collectibles shop. I sell some of this stuff over there."

"No shit?" He grinned, and she felt warmed by it. "That's awesome!"

She felt her cheeks heat. "Thanks."

"Do you ever sleep?"

"Not for a few weeks," she admitted. "That's the other reason I think it's better you sleep in my room. I have only a few weeks to finish this stuff up, and I don't know how late I'll be. It's better if I crash in here."

"Yeah," he admitted, looking sheepish. "That's... probably for the best."

"What, did you think I meant you should sleep with me?"

"Um..."

She started laughing, even as the thought made her heart beat a little faster. Sleeping next to Jericho? *Yes, please.* "No wonder you looked like you were cornered!"

"Hey, it wouldn't be that big a deal," he countered. "Remember when we both crashed on the inflatable mattress in your parents' living room when you made me watch a full marathon of that cartoon?"

"That was *Avatar: The Last Airbender,* and it was awesome," she said. "And yeah. Billy was off on a baseball thing, down in Los Angeles..."

"And your parents had gone with him, and my mom and I had a big fight," he said, his mouth tightening. She remembered that, too, now — he'd come over in the rain on his motorcycle, shivering because it was cold and he'd soaked through his jacket. She'd gotten out the huge air mattress, bundled him up, and then had fallen asleep watching hour after hour of the cartoon while eating kettle corn and drinking hot chocolate.

"Well, I'll probably just collapse in here," she said, wondering what it would be like to share a bed with him now. She got the feeling it wouldn't be quite as comforting. Impossibly, he seemed to carbonate her hormones even more now than he had when she was a teen. It had been nearly six months since she'd hooked up with anybody. Not that she'd minded. She suspected she must have a low sex drive or something, because given the opportunity to go out with a guy or stay in and sew or watch one of her shows... well, sewing won every time.

"Don't feel like you need to entertain me," Jericho said. "You've got this big project, and I can figure out what to do with myself." He paused on the way out, seeing the business cards she'd dropped on her worktable. "Summers Child Costumes, huh?"

"It's kind of a joke. It refers to *Game of Thrones*." She gestured to the Cersei season six finale dress she'd made. "That's what this is from."

He actually looked at it carefully, not just a quick, careless nod like she would've gotten from someone like Billy or, God forbid, Van Artist Guy. "That's badass. It's like a dress, but all tough and, I dunno, military-looking."

"You should see the badass bitch who wears it," she replied. "Ever seen the show? *Game of Thrones,* I mean?"

"Nah." He shrugged. "I don't watch too much TV — I hang out with the Machinists a lot. I'll catch football at a bar, sometimes."

"You'd like it, I think," she said. "You should try it. I have all the seasons on Blu-Ray."

He quirked an eyebrow.

"Come on. What else are you gonna do while I'm slaving away?"

"Actually," he said, "I thought I'd work out a little. Get out the kinks from riding up from Vegas."

"Oh. Okay. Well, clean towels are in the hall closet, and I'll, um, change out the sheets…"

"Don't worry, I got it," he said, and she could've kissed him for being considerate, even though she felt a stab of "bad hostess" guilt. "Do what you gotta do."

"In that case, I'm going to take a quick shower," she said. "I can't afford to get any grease or dirt on this fabric. Thanks!"

"Thank you for letting me stay here," he said with an amused grin.

She retreated to the bathroom, taking the world's quickest shower and changing into a T-shirt and shorts. She wrapped her blonde hair in a towel and then stepped out. "Bathroom's open if you—"

He wasn't wearing a shirt. He was just in a pair of shorts, doing push-ups on her living room floor, the rippling muscles on his back dancing in the low light. His profile looked intense, his body lightly misted with sweat.

Her mouth went dry, and damn it, her nipples turned to headlights under the thin fabric of her T-shirt.

"Lookin' good," she squeaked, then fled to the spare room. She mentally shook herself.

So much for her suspected low sex drive. One look at him and her engine was revving in the red. *Holy cannoli*, the guy was hot.

She bit her lip, then settled down to her sewing machine. She had too much to do to get sidetracked by a crush. The con was coming. Her friends were counting on her. And this would be a great opportunity.

As much as she liked Jericho, in a week or two, he'd be gone — and she'd still be here. She had more important things to focus on.

· ♥ · ♥ · ♥ · ♥ · ♥ ·

Jericho had never considered himself an insomniac before. He could usually sleep wherever, whenever. He'd slept in a tent in the Mojave and on a bench in Oklahoma; he'd slept on super-luxurious gel foam beds — with even more luxurious women — in Vegas; he'd crashed in a hammock on the beach at a Machinist's house in Florida. Generally, if he was tired, he stretched out, closed his eyes, and it would take an act of war to wake him up.

That said, he'd never slept at Kyla's place before, and he found himself rattled.

Not that it was uncomfortable. He had no idea why Kyla had such a huge bed — she was five foot four inches tall, tops — and the bed fit him comfortably. The sheets were really nice, too, and she had, like, a bajillion pillows.

But it had taken him a while to actually *get* to bed.

Part of it was feeling weird about putting her out, but she'd been softly humming along with whatever was in her earbuds.

Bored, he'd tried out *Game of Thrones* since Kyla had all the boxed sets. Normally the Dungeons-and-Dragons crap wasn't his thing, or at least, he didn't think so. But right from the jump, it was really exciting, with these creepy things killing this guy, and then another guy getting beheaded in, like, the first ten minutes. Zombie-like dudes with electric-blue eyes. It didn't lack for action, that was for damned sure.

Now that he was into it, there were all kinds of political things going on. He liked that Ned Stark guy. Ned seemed like the main character, and if that was the case, Jericho figured he'd enjoy seeing how the dude took charge as the series moved forward. He seemed to have his shit together, and was stand-up besides.

Jericho had finally felt exhaustion start to creep up on him at around midnight. He'd said good night to Kyla, but he doubted she heard him, as she was still humming and pinning away. He'd taken a shower and then curled up in bed, still feeling a bit guilty. It had taken him half an hour to finally go under.

The first thing he heard was a loud thump. It jogged at him, causing him to slowly surface.

Then, a voice, yelling. "*You are* such *an asshole!*"

He sat bolt upright, hands in fists, trying to get his bearings. Where the hell was he? Somebody was in trouble. Trouble was *here*.

He bolted out of bed, stubbing his toe on the nightstand and cursing. Kyla's house, he thought, still groggy.

Then, with cold clarity, he realized the person yelling was Kyla.

He couldn't have been more awake if he'd been dumped in a frozen lake. He rushed out of the room, shoving open the door of the second bedroom. It was dark, and it took his eyes a minute to adjust.

The bed was empty.

He almost punched out the dress form thing. Then he took a step and tripped onto the daybed after hearing Kyla's loud "oof."

"Kyla?"

He looked down.

There, on the floor, was Kyla. She was just wearing a nightshirt that had rucked up on her thighs, leaving her undies exposed. She was cradled on her arm, and she'd dragged some of the daybed's blankets down with her.

She also hadn't woken up. He hadn't stepped on her, thank God, but he had tripped and he'd hit the bed hard.

How the hell did she sleep through that?

"Asshole," she repeated, squirming.

He shook his head, feeling the adrenaline start to wear off. "I can't believe you're still sleeping," he said. "Kyla? Honey? You fell out of bed."

"Hmmm?"

He glanced. The daybed was miniscule, and that wasn't even counting the fact she had a bunch of crap on it. She'd been sleeping on maybe an eight-inch swath of bed, from the looks of it.

He sighed, then got down on the floor, jostling her a little. "Kyla," he murmured, stroking her cheek, not wanting to startle her. God, how the hell did she get her skin so soft? "Baby, you fell out of bed."

"No I didn't."

He smiled. "Yeah you did."

"No, *you* did." She sounded petulant, and rolled, presenting her back to him.

"You can't sleep on the floor," he said, trying for patience. "Your back will get all jacked up. Trust me."

"Go 'way," she muttered.

"Kyla," he said, more firmly, "I'm not letting you sleep on the floor."

She blew a raspberry at him.

"You have *got* to be awake," he muttered.

She didn't say anything.

"If you don't move your keister back onto the bed," he said... then frowned. Actually, she'd probably just fall off again. He considered the options.

That sofa of hers, maybe? But it didn't look that big, either. Or comfortable, really. He thought it might've belonged to her grandmother. There was a reason the Summers family was fond of inflatable beds.

What the hell was he supposed to do with her now?

Just put her in bed with you, a rogue thought shot forward.

His body tightened. He grimaced at himself.

The bed was big enough. He'd just sleep on top of the covers, that's all. That ought to keep her...

What, safe? Safe from what, exactly?

Well, it would keep her from being embarrassed, he reasoned. And tomorrow, they'd damn well talk over sleeping arrangements, because this was ridiculous.

He leaned down next to her ear. "I'm taking you to bed."

"Promises, promises," she slurred.

"You have *got* to be awake and messing with me," he muttered, then smoothed his hands over her, just a little, trying to figure out where her waist and legs were in the dark, where he could get a hold. Which was how he inadvertently discovered she had curves for *days*. He didn't touch anything that he shouldn't be touching — mostly just her back, her hips...

Okay, her butt. Once. But it was completely unintentional.

God, she has a great ass.

He hoped that didn't make him the asshole she was yelling about.

He put his arms under her thighs and her shoulder blades and then rolled her gently, picking her up like a rug. She turned into him, nestling against his bare shoulder. He felt her breasts pressing against him, with just the thin T-shirt material of her nightshirt between them.

Don't get any ideas, he counseled his dick. *This is not happening. This is off-limits.*

Carefully, he cradled her and stepped sideways out of the door, cautious not to bonk her head. He got her into her bedroom and then deposited her gently on the mattress.

Like a duck to water, she swam into the center of the bed, nestling instantly with a sigh as she snuggled into one of the multitude of pillows. She made a little happy hum.

"Greedy," he noted, then pulled a blanket up over her. He got onto the side of the bed. She was taking up a lot of the middle. He nudged her. Then he just took a breath and gently shoved her toward her "side" of the bed.

"Asshole."

"Yeah," he said, stretching out. She was out like a light, even if she did talk in her sleep.

There was the boundary of the cover between them. Even if there wasn't — even if he got under the thin blanket — he wasn't going to do anything. He slept like the dead — other women who had tried to seduce him awake had commented on it. He wasn't going to do anything stupid. And Kyla? Well, they might joke, but that *was* the joke. She was the least sexually forward person he knew.

Why are you so worried about this? Who are you trying to convince?

He frowned, closing his eyes. Why was he still mentally harping on this?

"Jericho?"

He opened his eyes, tensed. Feeling guilty. "Yeah, Kyla?"

"Iron Man is a total jackoff."

He burst out laughing. "The asshole you've been yelling about... is *Iron Man*?"

She snorted. "Fucker owes me ten bucks."

CHAPTER 3

Kyla awoke curled up against a mound of pillows... and a boulder. She winced in discomfort. She liked "nesting," as her family joked, surrounded by pillows that she could burrow into at any point. That said, even though some of her pillows had gotten kind of flat and probably needed to be replaced soon, she didn't have anything this hard.

Or warm, now that she thought about it. It was like sleeping on a furnace. She stroked her hand over the surface, slowly surfacing from sleep. What the hell was that, anyway?

She stretched out against it, yawning, still baffled. Smooth, she thought, then started to feel... crinkly. She vaguely remembered going to sleep on the daybed. The room was still dark — she had blackout curtains — and she figured she must've stretched out on some material.

Please, not the velvet, she thought, frowning. God, it'd take forever to get the wrinkles out.

She'd just meant to get a tiny little rest, then she'd clear off the daybed. Maybe it was the daybed itself? It was ancient, and the mattress was rock hard.

"You might not want to keep moving south, babe," a deep voice noted with obvious humor. She felt the voice under her ear, as well as...

Oh, shit.

She glanced up. Jericho had his hands perched behind his head, his shoulder-length dark hair looking tousled and sexy. He wasn't wearing a shirt. His dark brown eyes were twinkling with amusement.

She was also using his abs as a pillow, and her hand had been headed toward his waistband.

She threw herself off of him, landing on a pile of pillows. *"What the actual hell?"*

"Before you punch the crap out of me, a few things," he said, his tone punctuated by his rumbling laughter. "One: you are without a doubt the deepest sleeper I have ever met. Even more than me, and I've slept through gunfire."

She ignored him. "What are you doing in here? How are we even both on the day—" She stopped herself. "Wait, no. This is my bedroom. What am *I* doing in here?"

"Two," he continued when she paused, "you fell out of the daybed last night, and you were shouting. I about broke my toe getting in to make sure you were okay."

"Oh, God." She rubbed her hands over her face. "Sorry. I'm so sorry. I haven't done that in a while." As far as she could tell, she only talked in her sleep when she was particularly stressed and fatigued. She had been burning the candle from both ends.

"Three," he kept going as she felt her cheeks heating, "you had, like, half a foot of bed to sleep on in the spare room, so I figured if I put you back in there, you'd just fall out again. You also have the world's smallest, hardest couch, and I didn't want to jump out and check on you if you started yelling again. So I figured that you'd be better off in here."

"But how did I get in here?' she asked, still confused.

"How do you think? I carried you."

She felt her blush intensify. She wasn't exactly dainty. Then again, Jericho looked like he could bench-press a school bus. Man, she wished she'd been awake to enjoy getting carried to bed by him.

She'd only had a crush on him for how many years?

Oh, Lord. "Did I...I mean..." she started, then gestured downward. Almost immediately, she realized if she had done anything, there would probably be some sort of evidence.

Hard evidence.

She decided to not even *look* in that general area. If she blushed any harder, she'd probably set fire to the pillows. "I didn't touch anything I shouldn't, right?"

"I slept on top of the covers," he said. "Preserving both of our virtues, as it were."

Of course he did. And she'd simply clung to him like a frickin' unconscious barnacle. She burrowed her face into the pillows and groaned. "Well, your virtue was safe until I felt you up," she said, the sound muffled.

"Now that was hilarious, actually," he said, adding insult to injury. "It was like those cartoons, where you were obviously trying to figure out what the heck it was you were touching. Like when Jerry thinks he's hanging out with another mouse, only to reach back and realize what he's touching is the cat."

"Laugh it up, fuzzball," she shot back, scowling at him from over the edge of a pillow she clutched. "You're lucky I didn't maul you. It's been awhile. Any port in a storm, y'know?"

He cleared his throat, and she could tell he was trying not to chuckle. "Hil-a-rious," he repeated.

She felt... well... a mélange of emotions, really.

Relief that she hadn't embarrassed herself further, even though the sting of humiliation was still pretty sharp.

Layered on top of that was the stirring of her libido — she had a yummy huge guy beneath her fingertips, after all.

Finally, mortification that he was seeing the whole thing as "hilarious."

"I'll get the daybed cleared off tonight," she said, her words a little tense as she tried to process the confluence of emotion. "I'm sorry..."

"It's really not that big a deal," Jericho said. "I could use some covers next time, but you've got a bed like a football field. What does a little girl like you need with such a big bed, anyway?"

With any other man, that'd be considered innuendo, she thought ruefully. He just sounded genuinely puzzled. Of course, most other men wouldn't be calling her "little," either.

"I tend to move around a lot in my sleep," she said. "I like cool spots. So in the summer, I just sort of nomadically travel from one edge to the other."

"What's with all the pillows?"

"I also like to nest," she muttered. "I thought you were just another pillow. A hot, rock-hard, uncomfortable pillow."

He laughed out loud. "You're too cute."

She puffed up. "Well, if it's no big deal," she said with a huff, "I guess you won't mind just sharing. That daybed is, like, forty years old and needs a new mattress, and I could use the surface for the material, anyway."

As soon as the words were out of her mouth, she winced. *Stupid*, she chastised herself. She was already too aware of him just being in her apartment. But sharing a bed with him? What was she thinking? What was she *doing*?

His eyes widened. "Uh..."

She heard a knock on the door, and she sprung to her feet. She heard Billy's voice. "Hey! I brought breakfast!"

"Oh, crap. Oh, crap." She leaped out of bed and quickly threw on a pair of sweats, swearing under her breath. "Give me a sec!" she called out. She didn't dare look at Jericho.

She opened the door, hoping her hair wasn't too mussed.

Billy clumsily came in, his good arm caring a bag. He shut the door behind him with his foot. "Linds made breakfast burritos," he said, placing them on the kitchen table. "I figured we could eat before the day got started."

"That's nice of her," Kyla said. Was she out of breath? She sounded out of breath, didn't she?

God. She hadn't even *done* anything, and she felt guilty!

Jericho sauntered out, shirtless, in just his workout shorts. "Good morning, babe," he said, dropping a kiss on her cheek — and then lightly *slapping her ass.*

She jumped with a startled yelp.

Billy's eyes went round as he stared at them. Kyla held her breath.

Then, Billy started laughing uproariously.

"Good one, Jericho," he finally said, drying his eyes. "You guys suck, you know that? You almost had me going!"

Jericho grinned, winking at her. "Man, I'm hungry. She worked me out hard." With that, he swaggered to the kitchen table. "Breakfast burrito, huh? Smells good."

She grimaced, then headed to the kitchen table.

"Let me go get changed." She fled to her bedroom, locking the door and getting a pair of jeans and a T-shirt. She was pretty sure her cheeks were still flame red. When she finally cooled down, she wandered back out, where Jericho and Billy were still grinning and talking.

Jericho finished up his burrito. "Okay. I'm going to go take a quick shower. *Somebody* made me *work up a sweat* last night," he said, wiggling his eyebrows at her.

"Stop," she muttered, glaring at him.

Billy shook his head, his laughter subsiding and his eyes getting a little more stern.

Jericho grinned at her, then sauntered to the bedroom and grabbed some clothes, heading to the bathroom and the shower. He shut the door as Billy handed her a burrito.

She tucked into the burrito. Fortunately, Lindsay was a great cook. "Thanks," she said around a tantalizing mouthful of eggs, chorizo, and peppers. "This is really..."

"Why did you call him?" Billy interrupted, his expression serious.

She blinked, then swallowed. "What?"

He nodded at the bathroom, where they could both hear the shower running, and lowered his voice. "Jericho. Why did you call him?"

She was speechless for a second. "Because you're going to be out for a month, and I thought I could use the help...?"

"You could've managed," Billy said in a low voice. "I mean, it's not *that* bad."

She was shocked. "Why are you pissed at me?"

"I'm not pissed!" he hissed, then glanced at the bathroom again. "Sorry. I'm *not* pissed. It's just... it's kind of embarrassing, you know? You're a kick-ass mechanic. Hell, I've been out on plenty of vacations in the past year. You are more than capable of handling this."

"Believe me, I know," she said sharply. "Seeing as I *haven't* taken vacations!"

He huffed. "You could have. Don't put that on me."

She let out a squawk of indignation at this. "Are you serious? Remember when I told you I wanted to go to that con in Portland and you said that we'd be way too busy? Or that time—"

He glanced at the bathroom again. "That's not the point. Let's not get off topic."

She seethed.

He sighed. "Okay, I know I've been flaky. I know you can pull more than your share of the work. Which is why I don't know why you pulled Jericho into this. You *know* he hates this town. You know about his whole history here!"

She sighed. "It's been nine years, Billy."

"It's his mother, Ky."

She grimaced. Okay. Billy the Butthead might have a point on that one.

"And were you planning on paying him?" Billy pressed. "Do you know how much this guy makes doing custom work? I've seen his stuff. I think it's been featured in a few magazines. So you called him and asked him to come crash on your daybed and work for free because you're, what, tired?"

When he put it that way, she felt like a total jerk. She bit her lip.

"How long did you ask him to stay?"

"Not that long," she said hurriedly. "We didn't really discuss it. Maybe a week?"

"Keep it short," Billy said. The shower turned off, and Billy nodded meaningfully. "Don't take advantage," he added in a whisper.

"I'm not *trying* to take advantage!" she hissed back. "But I had plans! Stuff *I* need to get done. And taking care of the shop by myself for a month at least doesn't really help with that."

Billy, God help him, genuinely looked puzzled. "What?"

"*OtakuCon!*" she yelled, then gritted her teeth when he made the motion for her to quiet down. "It's less than a month away, and I still have tons to do!"

"Oh, that's all." He made a careless motion. "I thought, you know..."

"You thought what?"

He at least looked a little embarrassed. "I mean, I know it's important to *you*, but..."

Kyla felt her eyes well up with tears. She wasn't normally this emotional, she realized.

"Oh, kiddo," Billy said, his voice filling with alarm as he noticed. "Jeez. I didn't *mean* to break my arm. And there are other conventions you can go to, right? I promise, as soon as my arm heals up, you can go to one of those. Okay?"

She coughed slightly, clearing her throat, then brushed the tiny drops of moisture from her lashes.

"Don't be upset," Billy added.

I'm not crying because I'm upset, she thought. *I'm crying because I want to murder you, but I can't.*

Not that Billy would understand that. Frickin' idiot.

She closed her eyes, taking deep breaths. She focused on her muscle-tightening exercises. She made it through about twenty before she finally opened her eyes to see Jericho, his hair damp, looking at her with concern. Billy was also staring at her.

"Everything okay?" Jericho asked, looking only at her.

"Sure," Billy said instead. "All good. I'm going to go down and work on those invoices." He got up, shot Kyla a meaningful look, and then headed down.

Kyla sighed. Jericho stopped her before she could follow.

"Everything okay?" he repeated meaningfully.

No, she wanted to say. No, it wasn't. But she didn't want to guilt Jericho into staying. She hadn't thought this through. And she had no answers for her issues with Billy or the shop or the costume contest.

A few more deep breaths. A few more muscle clenches. Then she pasted on a megawatt smile.

"I'm fine," she said. "C'mon. Those cars aren't gonna fix themselves."

· ♥ · ♥ · ♥ · ♥ · ♥ ·

Jericho stared at Kyla's hyper-bright smile.

Fine, my ass.

He closed the door that Billy had left open and stood between it and Kyla, crossing his arms. "Okay, no bullshit. What's really wrong?"

"Nothing. It's all good," she said with a shrug, starting to walk around him.

"That might work on your brother, but you know that's not going to work on me." He stared her down. "What gives?"

Now she was frowning. "You're, what, holding me hostage up here? I don't want to talk about it."

"Obviously," he said, rolling his eyes, hoping she'd at least laugh at that. She didn't, crossing her arms to match his. "But I'm big, stupid and stubborn that way.

So come on, spill. You're upset or pissed or both. What happened?"

"Just drop it," she warned, her moss-green eyes going sharp. "I don't want to talk about it."

"Suppression isn't good for you."

"Standing between me and the door won't be good for you," she pointed out. "Did I tell you that I bought two Tasers?"

He sighed. "Sweetie, I'm not trying to be an ass here..."

"Yet strangely," she singsonged, "you're doing a staggering impression of one."

He stepped toward her, stroking her petal-soft cheek. "You looked like you'd been crying," he said. "Or about to. If you really want to brush it off, I will, but I worry about you."

She looked more startled than she had when he'd given her the playful smack on the butt. "You don't have to. I can take care of myself."

"I know that, believe me. And I know I don't have to," he said, cupping her face in his hands. She had this perfect heart-shaped face, the fine, light gold quality of her skin a counterpoint to his own tanned fingers. "I do because I *want* to. I've known you for years, and I came here to help. Are you upset because I'm here?"

"No!" she countered, then bit her lip.

Dammit. He suddenly remembered that little gesture. That was her tell. Whenever she was upset, she'd nibble at the corner of that rosebud lip. Funny how he'd forgotten that after being away for so long. "Shit. You are upset. Why? What'd I do?"

"You didn't do anything!" she quickly reassured him, shaking her head and resting her fingertips on his forearms. "Seriously. I mean, I was kinda wasted when I called you, and upset. I wasn't thinking clearly. I never should've asked."

He released her, feeling a little offended. "Why the hell not?" What, was he not good enough to help?

"Because... because you're, like, some custom-building badass super-mechanic!" she stammered, looking adorably flustered. "You've had your work in magazines, for pity's sake. And, like, auctioned for all this money. You've worked all over the country. Billy told me about it. You're a *big deal*!"

He chuckled. "Sweetie, it's only a big deal to a small group of people who are gearheads like us. It's not like I'm a rock star or anything. People don't see me walking down the street and start gaping at me going"—he pantomimed awe—"oh, my God, that's *Jericho Salomon, famous super-mechanic!*"

As he'd hoped, she finally laughed at that. His chest warmed. She was looking more cheered, less shaken. "Well, I'm sure they stare at you walking down the street," she said.

"It's the height thing, right?" he asked. "Six foot seven. It's like looking at Groot."

She nudged him. "More like 'who is Hottie McHotterson over there? Isn't he a rock star?'"

"Better," he said with a fake cheesy grin. "I *fix cars and motorcycles!*"

She sighed. "I'm sure you're making a hell of a lot on the custom builds especially. I didn't even think of that when I asked if you could come help. " She looked at the ground. "How much do..."

"I'm gonna stop you right there, before I get upset," he said in a low voice. "Don't talk about — don't even *think* about — offering to pay me."

She looked stubborn for a minute.

"What would your mother do if I told her I should pay her for all the holidays I spent here? All the nights I slept here?"

Kyla looked stunned. "I... I don't know."

"She'd slap the taste out of my mouth."

Kyla giggled. "Okay, I *know* she wouldn't do that."

"No, she wouldn't," he agreed. Mrs. Summers — Betty — was one of the sweetest women he'd ever met. She was the source of Kyla's megawatt cheerfulness. "But she'd say she was disappointed in me, then offer me pie or something. Somehow, it'd feel fifty times worse."

"Then my dad would kick your ass," Kyla added.

"As he should," Jericho agreed. Tom Summers, on the other hand, was where Kyla and Billy got their mechanical prowess — and their grit. A strong guy with a fierce temper, Tom was a man to be reckoned with. "The bottom line is, you and Billy are like family. If you need help, you're supposed to call me, okay?"

She sighed, then nodded. "I just hate feeling like I'm taking advantage of you."

"No, please," he teased. "Take advantage of me. Have your way."

She refused to be distracted. "You know. I'm yanking you away from your life."

"I don't know what kind of life you think I have," he said. "I left Snoqualmie because I didn't want an inside-the-box kind of life. I travel when I want to. I have my crew, the Machinists, but we're pretty loose. I travel with them when I want, work places when I feel like it, do whatever the hell I choose."

"No girlfriend?" she asked, then her cheeks pinked. "I mean... no apartment? No dog?"

"Not even a potted plant."

She looked somber. "There's a reason you haven't been back for nine years."

Now he stiffened. "Yeah," he said, shrugging.

"Have you spoken to her? Your mom?"

He rubbed his chin, avoiding Kyla's sympathetic gaze. "No," he admitted. "She told me to leave, and I've never gotten in contact since."

Kyla's lips pressed together, but she didn't say another word. "I didn't want you to come back here and get hurt," she said, looking down.

He sighed. "I know that. And if I thought it would be that painful, I wouldn't have come." Even as he said it, he realized he was lying. He owed the Summers too much, he reasoned. And he was twenty-six years old. It wasn't going to kill him to go back to the town where he was born. "I can handle it, okay?"

She sighed. "Okay."

"We good?"

"Yeah," she said with a smile. "We're good."

He held his arms open, and she moved into them, hugging him tightly. He wrapped his arms around her, tucking her head under his chin. She smelled good, he realized. That grapefruit body cleanser. She smelled like summer, the sharp sweetness of citrus, clean and bright like sunshine.

He pressed a quick kiss on the top of her head. "Anything else bugs you," he said against the crown of her head, "you talk to me, okay? None of this bottling-it-up bullshit?"

"Okay," she agreed.

"What is *taking* you guys so long?" Billy yelled up the stairs.

Jericho sighed, then opened the door. "We're having quick, wild monkey sex," he called back. "Can you give us a second?"

"*For God's sake*," Billy bellowed, and Kyla started cracking up.

· ♥ · ♥ · ♥ · ♥ · ♥ ·

The next few days went very well. Jericho was getting up to speed nicely, figuring out their maintenance and billing systems in a snap. "I've worked in at least ten different shops in the past nine years," he'd said with a diffident shrug when she showed how pleased and amazed she was at how quickly he caught on. "I can handle it."

"But I figured you'd just be doing, you know, the mechanic end," she said. "I can't believe you know the ordering systems and billing and stuff."

Jericho had seemed a bit embarrassed. "I don't know. It just didn't seem that hard."

Whether he admitted it or not, she was right. He was a frickin' *rock star*. They'd zipped through repairs and were even able to knock off a little early, waiting for parts that would be delivered on Monday.

If he could also sew and cook, he'd be the perfect man for her current predicament.

"You said 'the girls' are coming over for your costume thing, right? Do you want me to make myself scarce?" Jericho asked, looking at the door a little nervously. "I can go hang out with Billy and Lindsay. Or kill time at a bar or something."

He didn't sound enthusiastic about this. She knew that he probably didn't want to spend time in Snoqualmie itself, or North Bend — too many memories. It seemed even sillier for him to go farther away just to spend time at a bar with strangers. She knew he didn't like drinking, especially if he was riding. Besides, he'd hauled ass today. He'd probably be tired.

"It's up to you, but if you don't mind a bunch of women over, feel free to stay."

"How many is a bunch, exactly?" He looked skittish.

It was *adorable*.

She chuckled. "Just the Frost sisters tonight. If you want, you can shut yourself into my room. I can get *Game of Thrones* set up on my laptop, and you can watch it in there."

He smiled broadly. "I'm almost to the end of season one. You got me hooked."

She grinned back. There was nothing more gratifying than getting someone addicted to your favorite fandoms, she thought.

There was a knock on the door, and she answered it. Hailey and Rachel were waiting with broad grins.

She noticed their eyes open wide when they saw her house guest. "Jericho Salomon, I haven't seen you in ages," Hailey said, giving him a hug. Kyla felt a teeny, tiny little stab of jealousy, which was stupid. Because Jericho was just her friend, which everyone knew. It wasn't like they were a couple. Even if they were, Hailey was head-over-heels in love with her boyfriend, Jake. They were even talking about moving in together, which made sense considering she was always at his house anyway.

"Good to see you, Hailey," he said, then nodded at her sister. "You too, Rachel."

"You're motorcycling around, huh?" Hailey said. "Totally living the dream?"

Kyla mouthed at him: *Jericho Salomon, super-mechanic!*

He grinned wildly, causing her heart to race a little. "Something like that." He winked at Kyla. "Well, I'll get out of your way..."

"Give me a second," Kyla said to her friends, then tugged Jericho into her room. "Here. My headphones are noise-cancelling, and you can load the DVDs right here. If you need anything, let me know, okay?"

He nodded. "Thanks," he said as he put on the headphones.

She shut the door, only to find all the girls grinning at her expectantly. "What?"

"Jericho is staying here? *Sleeping* here? *In your room?*" Hailey said, doing a little victory dance. "Dish! How did this happen?"

"He's helping out at the shop for a little while," Kyla said. "Which, since Billy's going to be out of commission for a few weeks, is a lifesaver. Otherwise I'd probably be working at the shop until nine or ten every night, and I'd never get costumes done. Which reminds me — y'all better strip down and change."

"With him here?" Rachel yelped, then blushed. Hailey started laughing.

"Trust me," Kyla said, with a grin. "He won't budge from there with a crowbar. Women in packs probably scare him — or the costumes might. And he's been bingeing *Thrones* since he got here. I don't know how much sleep he got last night."

"How are the costumes going?" Rachel asked. If Hailey was the badass of the Frost sisters and Cressida the dreamer, Rachel was the queen: regal, determined, and cutting through the bullshit. "Is there anything we can do to help? You've done so much to help the store. If there's absolutely anything you need..."

Kyla sighed. "I love you guys, and I love helping you guys," she said, going into her workshop and putting on a wrist pincushion and pulling out the Megara dress, motioning Hailey in behind her. She talked to the others from the doorway as Hailey stripped down to underwear and tugged the dress over her head. "Let's be honest. I probably won't be able to meet the deadline on this costume contest. But this is a huge opportunity if I eventually want to make this costuming my livelihood."

"You could get a lot of new custom clients with the exposure from winning," Rachel agreed. Kyla could hear the rustling sound of the women getting down to underwear. Kyla motioned to Hailey to keep her arms up at an awkward angle.

"Don't stick me," Hailey warned her.

"Don't tempt me," Kyla quipped back, winking at her. Hailey snickered. "Okay. Just need to nip it in a little here... Damn. That sash isn't quite working. I want it to be more angular, like the movie." She bit her lip, her mind riffling through possible solutions. "I think I'm going to have to redo it. Build the sash with some cardboard to keep its shape."

"Is it really that important?" Hailey asked. "It's not that big a deal. Who's going to notice?"

Kyla blinked at her. "Do you know me at all?"

She made a few more adjustments, took a few more notes, and let the other women come in and look.

"That looks amazing," Rachel cooed. "I love the details. Are those brass?"

"Yeah. I welded those. And they're structural — actual dress pins, securing the shoulders," Kyla said with a small grin of pride. She'd done those first off, weeks ago, when she'd come up with the concept.

"You keep doing stuff like this, and that contest win is a *lock*," Hailey crowed.

Kyla's shoulders hunched. "It's just that level of attention that is going to kill me, time-wise," she admitted. "If I could spend the next three weeks *just* working on costumes, I might have a ghost of a shot of making it. But doing it just in the evenings?" She sighed. "Even with Jericho's help, it would be a miracle."

Not to mention Billy is still pissed that I asked Jericho in the first place. She wasn't sure how long Jericho was going to stay. She certainly wasn't going to ask him.

"And it'd be really hard to make a living at it. I don't mind working at the auto shop. I just... I hate that it takes up all my time. And that I seem to be the one who's running it, even though I have all these other things I want to do."

"Billy needs to step up more," Hailey snapped. "And you need to stop letting him run all over you."

"Hailey," Rachel reprimanded in a soft voice. The sisters exchanged glares.

"What? The guy goes off on vacations all the time. Fishing, skiing, camping. And you know he doesn't do all that invoicing and stuff, or any of the marketing," Hailey said. "Now that I'm working at the bookstore full time, I know how much that front-office stuff takes."

"Thank God," Rachel murmured, and Hailey shot her an evil look.

"Well, sorry I was too busy before, when I was *working two jobs* at the casino and the coffee shop..."

"Hey! Reclaiming my time, here," Kyla said before the sisters could argue more. "It's not that easy. Billy and I both agreed to take over the business so Dad and Mom could retire and travel around in the RV. They love it, and they're so freaking happy, it's fantastic." She unzipped Hailey, letting her step out of the dress before carefully putting it on the table and motioning Rachel forward with her muslin of the Liliana dress. Hailey got dressed as Rachel took her place on the stepstool, and Stacy leaned against the doorway. "Okay. This one's going to have a corset, but it's more like a modified pirate queen dress, except it'll be in royal purple. It'll go great with your coloring."

"You're not doing the boobalicious bra top with the short skirt?" Hailey said, sounding disappointed.

"Please, God, no," Rachel mourned, holding her hands out.

Kyla studied the drape of the fabric. It wasn't the final product — the satin she'd bought for this project had been expensive, but she'd learned the hard way not to skimp when working with the stuff. As a result, she wasn't making the muslin out of satin. Or out of actual muslin, for that matter. She'd found a cheaper fabric to make the prototype. She now realized that the paper pattern, and the dress form, had been a little off. "You lose some weight, Rachel?" she asked, making marks and adjustments.

Hailey stared at Rachel, who reddened. "Little bit," she said. "Finals are coming up."

Rachel worked her ass off. When Hailey was working two jobs — as a barista and a blackjack dealer — Rachel had worked essentially three. She was an event planner up at the nearby casino. She was responsible for the bookkeeping and the marketing plan for the bookstore. And, finally, she was finishing her MBA at night at the University of Washington. Kyla now felt a little bad about her own complaints.

"I now feel like a lazy lima bean," Kyla said. "Here I am, complaining…"

"No, I get it," Rachel said quickly. "And don't. I might burn the candle at both ends, but I love what I do. And school has a finish date. When I graduate, I'll be in an even better place to either take a new marketing job or do more with the casino and the bookstore. Or just work at the bookstore if we get big enough." Her voice all but thrummed with resolve. "I'm doing what I love. You're in a tough place because you love the people, but you're not loving the job so much anymore."

"And because Billy isn't pulling his weight," Hailey finished darkly.

Rachel gave Kyla a quick shoulder hug. "I don't have any advice to give, but I'm sorry," she said. "That sucks."

Kyla sighed. "I'll figure out something," she hedged. The truth was, the last thing she wanted to do was confront Billy. Worse, if she drew a hard boundary, she was afraid her parents would get involved. The Summers family was tight-knit. Her parents were the best people she knew. She was afraid if she told them they needed more help, or that she wanted to step back from the duties of being a mechanic and running the shop, that they'd stop RVing and her father would feel obligated to take the shop back over. She didn't want that for them.

She didn't know what to do, how to balance.

If only I had a little more time...

"I'll figure it out," she repeated, more to reassure herself than anything.

Suddenly, they heard a commotion from the bedroom. "Wait. Wait. *What?*" they heard Jericho yell.

"What the hell is that?" Hailey yelped.

"They *cut his head off?*" Jericho shouted.

Suddenly, the girls looked at each other and started laughing.

"If he's that worked up now," Rachel said, shaking her head, "just wait till he gets to the Red Wedding."

· ♥ · ♥ · ♥ · ♥ · ♥ ·

CHAPTER 4

It was one o'clock in the morning when Kyla finally stopped working on the dresses. The sisters had left around nine thirty. Jericho had wandered out long enough to share some leftover pizza with her after doing a workout that she had very virtuously ignored, going so far as to close the door... because, being honest, she was afraid she'd sew the dress to her own pants if she kept being distracted by Jericho's body.

Oh, my goodness, that body.

She put away the outfit and rubbed her eyes. She went into the bathroom and did her nightly routine, then stumbled to the bedroom. She was wearing a baggy T-shirt and a pair of boy shorts. She'd considered wearing yoga pants, but she hated sleeping in them — the shorts would be bad enough. Normally she slept in underwear. In the summer, she didn't even wear that much.

Maybe I should try that.

She groaned. God, she was tired if she thought dressing skimpy in front of Jericho was a good idea.

"You okay?" he rumbled.

The lights were dimmed. Jericho was already in bed, shirtless, of course. He closed up her laptop, putting it on her large nightstand. "I wasn't sure when you were going to come to bed."

Something about the way he said that — the unconscious intimacy — made her toes curl. "I was getting punchy," she said, exhaustion making her words slur together a little. "When I get this tired, it's dangerous."

"You might hurt yourself?" His looked her over with concern.

"Worse. Might fuck up the dress," she said, and he laughed with surprise. She collapsed face first on the bed. Probably not the sexiest of views — but hell, this was Jericho, and he probably thought she was about as sexy as a sack of marshmallows anyway. So screw it. "Heard you howling about *Game of Thrones*."

"I may not forgive you about season one," he teased. "But I'm getting through season two pretty quickly, so that's something. How much worse can it get, right?"

She thought about the stuff he had coming up — the roller coaster of the series, and all the deaths. "Yeah. Good luck with that."

"Oh, really?" He raised an eyebrow. "Maybe I should pull out now, while I can."

"Hah. You're addicted, just like the rest of us," she scoffed. "That was my plan all along. Bwa ha ha."

He stared at her. "What's wrong? You're wincing, and you're scrunched funny and rubbing your shoulder."

"Sewing too long," she said. "Should've gotten up and stretched periodically, but I was on a roll."

"And you put in a full day in the garage, too," he said. He cleared his throat. "Want me to rub that down?"

She felt a little thrill.

"Nothing weird or, you know, skeevy," he said quickly. "This is purely physical therapy."

"Of course," she demurred, feeling stupid. Of course it would be nothing more than therapeutic. They didn't have that kind of relationship. Honestly, if another man had offered her a massage out of the blue, she'd probably be pretty grossed out. Of course, she wouldn't be sharing a bed, even platonically, with just anyone.

And Jericho was far from just anyone.

"Where do you want me?" she asked.

He paused for a second, and she figured he was trying to figure out the best location. The bed really was pretty big. She'd gotten super California King and had to make all her sheets herself, but it was worth it. "Why don't you get on this side, and I'll stand?" he finally said.

She waited for him.

"Lie on your stomach," he instructed her. "I'll get up in a second."

She shrugged, then did as he instructed. "Don't tickle me," she warned. "Seriously. I will kick you."

He chuckled softly. "Duly noted."

When he put his palms on her shoulders, she sighed. When he started working her shoulders, it was all she could do to hold back a moan. "Holy crap, you are good at this."

"Jericho Salomon, super-mechanic and part time masseur," he said, and she let out a sound that would've been a laugh if she weren't so frickin' tired. "You really have been pushing yourself hard, huh?"

She made a noncommittal sound. "Mrmph."

"Why?"

"The shop needs me."

"No. Why the costumes?"

She sighed. She hoped this wasn't going to be another Billy-esque conversation. "Because I love it. I've loved playing dress-up since I was a kid. I like making clothing, sure, but it's the fantasy, you know? I didn't just want to make stuff to wear to school or for other people to... I don't know, go to work, wear to parties. I love elves and swords and sorcery and escaping into stories. Clothing helps me do that."

He was still rubbing her shoulders, and she could feel herself unwinding into a puddle. It was so good she wanted to purr. "Do you work this hard on all the... what are they called? Shows?"

"Conventions. Cons," she responded. "I— Ouch!"

He immediately stopped. "Sorry," he said quickly. "Damn, girl. You are really, really tight."

"That's what I've heard," she quipped quickly, then winced again. "Sorry. It's late, I'm tired, my filter's shut down for the night."

He didn't say anything, just continued to rub, more gently this time.

She sighed. She must've embarrassed him. She guessed it was one thing to wind Billy up, another to flirt and joke just between the two of them. "Anyway, this con is a little special," she continued, trying to quickly get back on track. "There's this contest. There's some prize money, but if I won, I'd be included in a big catalog and get great publicity. It'd be a jumping-off point."

"For what?" he asked. Her neck slowly succumbed to his tender ministrations, turning to putty beneath his fingers. She sighed with pleasure.

"For starting a costume business... Oh, God, that feels fantastic," she moaned.

He paused. "You want to start another business?"

She tensed.

"No, no," he said, stroking her quickly. "You'll ruin all my hard work. Would this be like a sideline thing? Like, alongside the shop?"

He was working down her sides, his thumbs pressing into her hips and her lower back, releasing the knotted muscles. She groaned, twisting slightly as pain was released. "Ideally? I'd love to make it a full-time thing," she said. "It would be a dream come true. But it's rare. I don't know anybody who works at costuming full time. It's like running away to join the circus or something."

He leaned over. She could feel the heat from his chest, smell the clean, masculine scent coming off of him. "Or joining a motorcycle club, right?"

"People do that all the time," she protested.

"Scoot over," he instructed, and she did, rolling a little. He stretched out next to her. His dark brown eyes gazed deeply into hers, intense. "Ky, do you want this costume thing?"

She shrugged.

"No bullshit. Do you want this?"

Maybe it was the lateness of the hour or how tired she was, but she sighed. "Yes."

"You should always go for what you want," he said. "Trust me. I know how much it sucks to try to be what you're not just to make people happy. Even if you love those people. Understand?"

She swallowed. It was like he was looking deep inside her.

"Now, when is this convention thing?"

"In three weeks."

He looked to the ceiling, like he was doing some calculations. "I've got a thing in Idaho I have to do in about that time," he said. "But I think I could stay until you're done."

"Really?" She felt her heart speed up.

"And in that time," he said, chucking her chin up so she kept looking at him, "I don't want you down in the garage. You're just gonna work on the costumes."

"Oh, no!" she quickly protested, sitting up. "No, I couldn't. You didn't come here to..."

"I came here to help you," he said, sitting up, too. "Not watch you kill yourself trying to do too much. You don't have that hard a system, and no offense, but I've worked in busier shops. You think I can't handle Summers Auto?"

She sighed. "Of course you can," she said. "Obviously. But..."

"But what?"

"I don't know. It just feels wrong!"

He laughed. "Tell you what. I'll wrestle you for it. If I win, you stay out of the shop. If you win, you can keep doing both. Deal?"

She looked him over. "You're like an oak, dude." And damn, wouldn't she like to climb that tree?

Okay, now was not the time to take a walk down that particular memory lane in crushville.

"So you're saying you concede." He smirked.

She hated smirks.

Without warning, she leaped on him, reveling in the look of surprise on his face as she landed across his chest. "Pinned!"

"You need, like, a three count," he said, and quickly reversed their positions. She was on her back, and he was gently pinning her shoulders. "One... two..."

She struggled, wiggling and writhing — and laughing. She pinched the sensitive skin on the underside of his arm, by his armpit. Yelping, he released her, giving her room to escape.

"Cheating!"

"I learned from the best," she said.

He turned on her, his eyes gleaming. "Now you're gonna get it."

She couldn't help it. Even as she was laughing, her body was incredibly turned on. "You talk big," she shot back. "But I'm thinking it's all show."

With a low roar, he reached for her hips, tugging her until she fell back on the mattress. She started wriggling like crazy, bucking and pinching. "Not gonna fall for that twice," he gasped.

In a frozen moment, she took stock of the situation. He was looming over her, his shoulders flexing, his body lightly gleaming. The dimple in his cheek pitting.

Her heart stopped. He was dominant, gorgeous — and propped up over her.

Then, in a second, he collapsed, smooshing her.

"Gack!" she yelped. "You're... squishing... me!"

She felt more than heard his chuckle. "Do you yield?"

"Yes! Okay! I give!"

He rolled off her quickly. "Six foot seven, baby," he said, his tone utterly smug. "Don't bring a knife to a gun fight."

"I may be small, but I'm wily," she countered. "And I know where you sleep."

"Ha." He shut off the light. "Speaking of... get some rest, babe. You've got a full day of costume-making tomorrow."

She scrunched down on the bed. Her heart was still racing. Sure, he'd turned it into a joke... but for a second there, the weight of him, the feel of him, was everything her body had wanted. She just wanted to sink her teeth into him. She wanted to feel his hands, so rough and yet so gentle, exploring every inch of her.

God, she'd thought she'd put this crush behind her. But no, now she was finally sharing a bed with the man she'd been in love with for years — and he was treating her like a kid.

Some things, it appeared, never changed.

One hour later, Jericho was lying in Kyla's bed, unable to sleep.

She seemed to be asleep. Actually, she seemed to be knocked-out-by-Mike-Tyson-unconscious. She'd been working herself ragged, and it all caught up with her.

You shouldn't have touched her, dude.

He'd only wanted to help her feel better. She was wound like a spring and just seemed so beat up, so exhausted. So he'd given her a rubdown. Granted, he wouldn't have offered one to any of his male friends — the idea of him telling Pedro, *hey, you seem stressed, let me work those shoulders,* would have probably made all of them uncomfortable — but Kyla was a touchy-feely person. She hugged. She snuggled. She gave the occasional arm-punch. And she brought out the touchy-feely in him, too. And she was genuinely hurting. If Billy had sprained his ankle, for example, he would totally look it over and wrap it up.

It was a medical thing, he reasoned.

But the wrestling — now, that was pure stupidity on his part.

He ran a hand over his face. Again, if they were still kids, it wouldn't have been that big a deal. But they weren't kids. Her body, and his body's reaction to her body, was more than enough proof of that. His dick was still half-cocked and resentful. He was lucky he'd turned it silly when he had and rolled the hell off of her.

He was here to help. Not to hit on. And certainly not to hit it. Kyla was one of his oldest friends, *and* the little sister of one of his oldest friends. If he had mindless sex with Kyla, Betty Summers might actually move from disappointed to murderous — and Tom Summers would probably destroy whatever Betty left over.

Beyond that, even if the Summers family connection weren't there, there was no way he was going to stay in Snoqualmie, with all the memories and his family still living here. And the Machinists still needed him. No, there were way too many obstacles for him to consider anything as permanent as a relationship, and Kyla deserved a relationship, and he wasn't cut out for that sort of thing. He was short term at best.

He blinked. And he wasn't quite sure why he was arguing with himself about this. He'd just wrestled a little with an old friend who happened to be a girl, that's all. He got a little stirred up. He hadn't hooked up in a while. No need to dissect it.

Still arguing with yourself, dude.

He grimaced, then picked up his phone to check the time. Two fifteen a.m. He really needed to get some sleep himself.

A blinking light caught his attention. Texts, he realized, from Mike, Pedro, and Trevor. He'd been ignoring them, and they had started to accumulate. He groaned, then started scrolling through.

Mike: When are you getting back? We need to talk. Trevor's right — we're getting big. Need to think about doing something different.

Mike: Especially with this many new people.

Mike: Don't want it to be gangsta MC, though. Maybe AMA?

Jericho blinked in surprise. AMA — the American Motorcycle Association — was a respected and structured organization. If they made the club an AMA-sanctioned group, it would mean a lot of paperwork, but it might be a good way to organize all the new people who were finding out about them. It would probably make it a lot stuffier, though. Jericho grimaced, then shifted to Trevor.

Trevor: Dude, when the hell are you getting back? Mike wants to pull some BULLSHIT.

Jericho sighed.

Trevor: AMA? Those pussies? We could be a real club. We have the numbers, and you know we got the interest.

That was true, actually. There were plenty of kids, new recruits, who were gearheads, interested in the mechanics of the club. But that didn't take away from the mystique. They were auto nerds who wanted to be seen as badasses. What Trevor was proposing might be a draw for a lot of them. Jericho wasn't sure how he felt about that.

Trevor: We need to talk before the rally, get this shit locked down.

Jericho shut the message, suppressing a groan. Actually, the last thing he wanted to do was talk about this shit right now. He was enjoying himself in Snoqualmie, hard as it was to believe. He wanted to take a break from the Machinist drama until Rally.

Apparently, Pedro shared the thought, since his lone message was: *If Mike and Trev don't shut the hell up, I am going to choke out both of them.*

Jericho let out a bark of laughter, then shot a quick glance at Kyla, who stirred. She'd been on her stomach, nestled in her mountain of pillows. Now, she flipped over, giving him a better view of her face, framed in a mess of curls. She made a sound of protest.

"Sorry," he whispered, studying her. Had he awakened her?

She arched her back, and he felt his soft question die in his throat. In the dim light from his cell phone, he saw her stretch like a cat, shifting her hips, her curves mesmerizing. Her T-shirt was thin, and he could make out the bumps of nipples pointing up through it on top of her significant breasts, the areolas creating tantalizing shadows beneath the thin white cotton. Her boy-shorts rode low, the gentle pooch of her stomach transitioning to generous hips and thighs before disappearing beneath the thin covers.

He stared.

She started to move, her thighs rubbing together as she made a restless sound, her arms splayed out.

His mouth watered. She tilted her head, exposing the sweet connection of her neck to her jawbone and the delicate spot just beneath her ear. He wanted to nibble there, see what it tasted like. Breathe that scent of citrus and woman who was—

This is Kyla! What the fuck is wrong with you?

He brought himself up short, realizing that his breathing had gone shallow. Yes, he knew it was Kyla. But all of his excuses paled in comparison to the reality of the woman in front of him, apparently asleep, but shifting and gyrating to some kind of erotic dream.

"Mmmmm," she breathed, and turned to her side, facing away from him. Good God, that ass, he thought, as his cock went from half-mast to straight-up midnight. Just *all* of her. The way she moved, even in sleep.

What would it be like? he wondered.

His phone shut off, and she disappeared into the darkness. He immediately felt a pang of desolation. Then he heard her.

"Mmmm... Oh..." Her breathing was speeding up, too, he realized.

What was she dreaming?

His mind was going crazy with imagining. He could hear her body sliding and shifting over the bedsheets. He could hear the sound of her rounded nails gently raking over what he thought was a pillow, then a soft sound.

What *was* that?

Gritting his teeth, unable to stop his curiosity, he turned on the phone again.

Her hips were gyrating, her skin sliding along the fabric. She had one hand in her hair — and one smoothing over the front of her boy-shorts. That's what he was hearing. Her dampness, the motion...

He held his breath. She was breathing hard, fast. He realized his squirming was matching hers. He refused to touch her, or himself, but he'd be damned if he was able to tear his eyes away from the vision that he was watching.

"Unh... oh... oh, *God*... " she breathed. Mentally, he was urging her on. This was the hottest thing he'd ever seen in his life.

Was she going to come?

He really, really hoped so. Hell, he was ready to go, and he hadn't even touched himself. He hadn't felt like this since he was a teen.

"*Oh!*" She let out a soft cry, then started to tremble, her hips twitching, her thighs clenching and releasing. He thought he saw the sheen of wetness between them.

Then the room went dark again.

He couldn't help it. He got up and headed for the bathroom, stripping off his clothes and jumping into the shower. He didn't even give the water a chance to heat up. It didn't matter. He took himself in hand. He could've fucking driven a railroad spike with his cock at that point, and he was *trembling*.

Didn't matter. Two strokes, three, and he was already shuddering, shooting his load into the tub.

He leaned against the cold tile, shaken by what he'd witnessed. Kyla. Who would have guessed?

And how was he supposed to share a bed with her now, without thinking of that?

· ♥ · ♥ · ♥ · ♥ · ♥ ·

The next day, Kyla sewed like a woman possessed.

It felt weird to be upstairs in her apartment, sewing, as she heard the sounds of the shop whirring and buzzing below her. She'd put on her headphones and focused for the better part of the morning, but now it was getting close to lunchtime. She'd gotten an amazing amount of work done, especially considering how fuzzy-headed she felt. She hadn't gotten to sleep until one o'clock, and she'd gone under like a tidal wave had hit her. But she wasn't exactly well-rested. She'd had a super-sexy dream of Jericho. He'd been shirtless, wearing only his workout pants. Then he hadn't been wearing the workout pants.

"Hey, babe," he'd said, and swept her up in bed. She got the feeling it was in some luxurious, unbelievable place — hell, it might've been a cloud for all she knew — and then he'd...

She felt the blush smack her, even though she was all alone in her apartment. He'd gone to town, she thought.

And he'd done it *well*.

It had all started to blur together at some point. All she knew was, he'd used his mouth and his... well, other parts, he'd lavished attention on every inch of her, and he'd made her feel like a frickin' sex goddess. His kisses were drugging. His hands were magic.

And most amazing of all: she'd managed to have an orgasm.

She'd heard that some women had orgasms in dreams all the time. She didn't know who these miracle women were. All she knew was, when she dreamed of sex, or tried to, it usually culminated with her trying to find a place to actually have sex (usually in a hallway of locked doors) or getting interrupted by people like her family or a parade of customers or, in one unfortunate but memorable instance, a SWAT team.

She was sure a therapist could and would have a field day with this.

The bottom line was, she'd been with Jericho. She'd come hard enough that her ears were still ringing when she woke up that morning. And she was wondering whether she'd be in a state of permanent blushing when he came back upstairs.

She'd actually slept in that morning. She hadn't heard him get up and go downstairs. It wasn't until the garage doors had opened and she'd heard the hydraulic lift operating that she'd started to surface. She *never* woke up that late. Her initial state of sexy bemusement had quickly gotten swept away with panic — *oh shit, I'm late for work!* — when she'd found Jericho's note for her on the pillow next to her.

Remember: you stay up here and get those costumes done. I'll be up for dinner. Good luck.

He hadn't signed the note, of course. Why would he? Who else was sharing her bed?

At which point she'd quickly gotten the chills from her remembered dream sex. She'd taken a cold shower.

After which she'd forced herself to put her head down and focus on work.

By twelve thirty, her stomach was yowling. She was about to forage for some food, realizing she'd skipped breakfast, when Jericho walked in.

"How's it going?" He sent her a lopsided half smile.

Her heart zoomed into overdrive, as did her hormones. "Good," she said automatically. "Really good. I've got the Megara costume done, and I'm making good progress on Liliana. I need to double-check with the costume contest people to make sure I'm covering all the categories, but I think that it'll go well."

"Good." He was still smiling at her, but there was something...different. A glow in his eyes. A certain intensity.

Maybe that's because you're looking at him through dream-sex glasses. A nice big "O" would alter any girl's perceptions.

She cleared her throat, quickly looked away, and pressed her thighs together.

"You've got some asshole customers, though," he added. "This one guy wanted to haggle over how much we charged. Especially since we didn't offer extra 'amenities' and didn't offer him delivery. Total douchebag."

She sighed. "GMC van owner? Wears a beanie?"

"Yeah. You know him?"

She shrugged. "He was kind of a sexist asshat when he dropped it off. Was looking for the mechanic — a man, obviously, not a woman like me."

She couldn't help but notice that Jericho looked her over quickly, lingering on her chest just a second after she said *woman*. His eyebrow went up. "And you didn't kill him?"

"Nope. I did my patented calming technique, went hyper-cheerful, and sent him on his way."

Jericho moved closer, all but whispering in her ear. "Someday, you gotta teach me this technique of yours."

She shivered. *I'd love to teach you muscle-tensing and relaxing techniques.* Which only brought back memories of last night's dream.

"Do you really want to know?" she quickly asked, heading off that avenue of thought.

"Yeah, I do." He smiled at her.

"Promise not to tell anyone?"

"Who am I gonna tell?" She could tell he was trying not to laugh. "Okay, I promise."

Now she was dying with embarrassment. What was she thinking? Leaning forward, she buried her head against his chest, then muttered, "I do kegels."

She felt him stiffen. "You... eat bagels?" he asked.

She started snickering, then giggling, then laughing even harder, until he laughed along with her, lightly looping his arms around her.

"Not bagels," she corrected, breathlessly, her cheeks hurting from smiling. "I do *kegels*."

He blinked, leaning back to stare at her. "You do... kegels?" he repeated.

"When I get stressed out, or a customer pisses me off, or I get mansplained by some douchebag cosplay guy or something," she whispered. "I just smile like Pollyanna on meth and do kegels until the desire to strangle them passes."

He stared at her for a long moment, and she wondered if he was shocked or uncomfortable, until *he* started laughing, much like she had. In fact, he'd released her and was doubled over, leaning against a wall. "Oh, my God," he said, wiping at his eye. "You are too much. Really. You are nuts."

"Sure, laugh now," she said, poking him in the midsection and looking up at him, her eyes bright with mischief. "But someday I'll be a Zen monk who can bend a metal bar with her hoohah, and who'll be laughing then, huh?"

Jericho's brown eyes shone, and he stroked her face. It took everything in her not to curve into his palm like a cat. "You are one of my favorite people," he told her, his thumb tracing the apple of her cheek. "You know that?"

"Well, isn't this cozy," a new voice interrupted.

Jericho and Kyla turned at the same time, releasing each other.

There was a blond man standing in her doorway. He was wearing riding leathers, and his jacket was dark, a bombers' jacket. He was wearing a Machinist T-shirt, although he didn't fill it as well as Jericho. He looked younger than Jericho but harder somehow. He pushed his sunglasses up on his forehead, his gaze crawling over Kyla like a centipede. She took an instinctive step back.

Jericho stepped between them. "What the hell are you doing here, Trevor?"

"I wanted to check out the emergency that dragged you out here," Trevor said. "We're like family, after all. If it affects you, it affects us." He held out his hand to Kyla. "Trevor Jackson."

"Kyla Summers," she said, shaking his hand. She realized she was just in a pair of yoga pants and a T-shirt, and took an unconscious half step behind Jericho again.

"Kyla. Your brother broke his arm, huh?" Trevor continued, his voice outwardly conversational. "Talked to him downstairs. He said you're staying here, Jericho."

There was nothing overtly suggestive about his statement, or really anything he was doing, but Kyla's instincts were still going off like a fire alarm. There was something off about this guy, she thought. Nothing obvious, but not something she could ignore, either.

"You couldn't wait until I got to Idaho?" Jericho's voice was frigid with disapproval.

Trevor shook his head. "You were ignoring my texts. I've been doing a lot of arguing with Mike and talking with Pedro. I've got ideas for the club, but you guys are the ones running it. If you're not on board, you're not on board — I get that. But I want to talk to you about it. Okay?"

Jericho looked like he wanted to argue. Actually, he kind of looked like he wanted to punch Trevor out. Then he sighed.

"Not here," he said, and he shot her a glance of warning. "Come on. We'll grab some lunch."

"You got it." Trevor smiled. "Nice to meet you, Kyla."

She nodded, even though she didn't agree. Jericho sighed as Trevor headed down the stairs. "I think we'll hit Herfy's," he said. "You want anything? Burger or shake?"

"Is everything okay?" she asked instead.

Jericho's expression was drawn. "Yeah, sure," he said. "Don't worry about it. I won't be long."

She sighed, too. "Oreo shake," she requested.

"You got it." With that, he descended the stairs, shutting the door behind him.

She looked out the window, watching as he got on his bike. Trevor got on another bike. There was a third man, a rough giant who looked like a walking cliff-face with a thick walnut brown beard and matching, eyebrows. He made Jericho look diminutive.

For the first time, she wondered what the hell Jericho was into... and what he was walking away from to help her out.

CHAPTER 5

"So... this is Snoqualmie," Trevor said, looking out the windows of the small burger joint. "Wasn't expecting it to be quite so, y'know, bumfuck nowhere. There are a *lot* of trees around. Kinda spooky."

"Well, they did film *Twin Peaks* around here," Jericho said, his voice flat.

Trevor looked at him blankly. "The fuck is *Twin Peaks?*"

Which reminded Jericho: for all his tough attitude, Trevor was still, essentially, a kid. He couldn't be much more than twenty-three or twenty-four, tops. He liked to get involved, liked to run things. Thought of himself as a leader. God knows, he'd pushed his way into a "leadership" position at the Machinists somehow. Even though it was Mike's son who had boosted membership with the improved website and promotion, it was Trevor who had somehow become a public face for the Machinists at biker bars and rallies, especially with the new kids. Jericho probably should've said something about it a while ago, but he'd figured live and let live. He was loyal to Mike and Pedro, and he liked helping a young guy come up.

Now, Jericho was wondering how big a mistake that might've been.

"Why don't you tell me what you're really doing here," Jericho said as they waited for their food to arrive.

Jericho looked at Trevor's little brother, Connor, who, not surprisingly, remained silent. Jericho hadn't heard the guy say a word in the two or three years he'd know the brothers. And by *little*, it had to mean younger, because Connor was built like a tank. Rumor had it he was big brother Trevor's enforcer. Connor was a gifted mechanic on his own, but he was a package deal: you worked through Trevor or you got nothing. Jericho got the feeling that if Trevor told Connor to step into traffic, Connor would choose an eighteen-wheeler to leap in front of, just to try to impress him. There was also a good chance Connor would simply take out the semi.

The fact that Trevor had brought Connor with him for this little conversation put Jericho on edge.

"You wouldn't answer your phone, wouldn't return texts," Trevor said with a shrug. "We need to talk. You know the club's getting big. We're getting more members every week. Mike's kid says we're up to a few hundred and getting email from all over the country."

Jericho shrugged. "So? We never meant for this to become a thing. It was just fun. Just, you know, us."

"Yeah, well, Mike was the one who put the T-shirts up on the website, and I'm the one who started selling them at rallies. And wasn't it your idea to hook up the shops you were working at with Machinist approved signs and shit?"

"That was a joke," Jericho grumbled. "Sort of. And it turned into a thing."

"I know. I've heard the story. Pedro had a friend in a custom shop who needed a mechanic, and you went cross country to work in North Carolina. Then another guy wanted a custom bike, but he needed it done in a shop in Philly. Next thing you know, you're working in Arizona and Texas and Oregon. The Machinist network."

"They're good shops." Jericho felt both embarrassed and puzzled. "And what does this have to do with anything?"

"We know our shit, that's what." Trevor ignored the waitress as she put their burgers and fries down in front of them. "We build the baddest bikes in the business."

Jericho couldn't help but look at Trevor skeptically, then at Connor, who seemed to be ignoring the conversation, dredging a fry in ketchup. "That still doesn't tell me why you want to turn it into a fucking fraternity on wheels."

"Nothing that pussy," Trevor said, glaring. "A club. A true MC."

Jericho had been afraid that was where this was going. "No. *Hell* no."

"We're practically a club anyway," Trevor said, his expression surprisingly earnest. "Think about it. Pedro started us — he's the president and VP rolled up in one. Mike handles any money stuff that comes up, and he's the one who set up the website and handles group texts and shit when we go on group rides. And you're the sergeant-at-arms. You make sure that nobody steps out of line when we rally. It's *just* like a club."

"Wouldn't know. Never been in a motorcycle club."

"Trust me, the Machinists are the same thing. They just don't wear colors."

"So why do we need to get official?" Jericho pointed out. "Again, we're doing fine."

"Are we, though?" Trevor shook his head. "Y'all are spread too thin. Mike's got a business, for Christ's sake. Pedro's got a kid in junior high or some shit. And we don't have a road captain. It's just this side of a clusterfuck. We've gotten this far on sheer luck."

"If people don't like it, they don't have to be a part of it." Now Jericho wondered if he was being sulky.

"You were a kid when you joined," Trevor said. "You've said how important the club has been to you. We're like family. The Machinists are my family now."

Now Jericho felt like a shit. "I do feel that way," he admitted.

"We've got new guys coming up, who want to learn, who want to be a part of something bigger," Trevor said persuasively. "Don't you want to give that to them? Don't you want to offer them a chance?"

Jericho sighed. "We're not gonna become one per-centers," he said, his voice sharp. "No colors, no patches, none of that bullshit."

"We wouldn't have to be that hard-core," Trevor hedged.

"No, Trevor."

"There are already guys who are dipping a little on the wilder side. You know it, I know it. Pedro knows it."

"I said *no*."

Jericho was loud enough that the woman working the counter, the cook, and the construction workers who had come in for food were staring at them.

He took a deep breath and lowered his voice. "The guys know where I stand on this. And it's not like you have a say."

Trevor smiled. "Don't I? The shops listen to me now, too. A lot of the guys listen to me."

"So what? Pedro and Mike set up the club."

"Mike and Pedro set it up, yeah, but they told people they were members. So if Mike wants this to be all AMA, people are going to have votes one way or the other. And if they don't want that..." Trevor's smile was predatory. "Maybe we just take the name and the connections and do what the fuck we want anyway."

Jericho felt his hands ball into fists. "Sounds like you've already made your decision."

"I'm just giving you a heads-up." Trevor said, his voice just this side of smug. "While you're playing house here in East Nowhere, the club's going to make a choice, with or without you. I think you'd be good on the team. Just figure out which way you want to go with it. It's not like you've been a choirboy, either." Now Trevor leered. "Speaking of... who's the thick blonde? Man, she has got a *rack* on her. And that ass..."

Jericho got to his feet and grabbed Trevor by the collar, yanking him out of the booth.

"Hey!" the cook yelled. "Don't make me call the cops!"

Trevor still grinned despite Jericho's grip. Connor got to his feet, shorter than Jericho but stockier, built like a bunker. He didn't seem to like confrontation, but when it came to Trevor, he didn't flinch from it, either.

"We'll talk in Idaho, at the rally," Jericho said. "Now get the fuck out of here."

He grabbed Kyla's shake and headed for his bike. Trevor and Connor trailed him.

"Just remember: I'm going to be talking to the riders themselves while you're out here. You're going to be outnumbered," Trevor said. "I'd rather have you on my side."

"Fuck off," Jericho muttered inside his helmet, then rode off, back to the shop. He was going to have to do something about Trevor. There were too many new kids in the Machinists, too many good people involved for a cocky kid who wanted to be a gangster biker to screw up. He'd text Pedro and Mike, he thought. But he knew to make a real impact, he was going to have to go talk to people.

As soon as I'm done, he reasoned. *As soon as I leave.*

He felt a little stab of regret. He always knew he was going to have to leave, after all. Just a couple of weeks.

He just hadn't realized he was going to feel this much regret.

· ♥ · ♥ · ♥ · ♥ · ♥ ·

Kyla was trying to focus on sewing and not focusing on scary looking bikers when Billy came upstairs.

"You're still working on this stuff?" Billy asked, sounding exasperated. "How long is that supposed to take?"

Kyla gritted her teeth. She was too anxious to do muscle exercises or deep breaths, especially when dealing with her brother seemed to take twice the emotional fortitude than dealing with anybody else. "I made a deal with Jericho, remember? He'd man the shop, and I'd get this stuff done in time for OtakuCon."

"Yeah, well, he's been gone for almost an hour," Billy pointed out. "And we're backlogged."

She glared at him. "You didn't take on any new big projects, did you?"

"Nothing major," he said, but looked away. "But come on, Ky, be real. We can't go without customers for three months."

"I don't want engine rebuilds and custom stuff. If it's routine, we can take it. And we've got some cushion for emergencies."

"What, dig into savings?" Billy rolled his eyes. "What, do you want Jericho just standing around? Or the shop losing money because you're in here making princess dresses?"

"*No new clients*," she said emphatically. "Jericho's just here to handle the backlog and keep us up to date, not to get swamped and dragged into some major builds. I mean it, Billy."

"Well, it wouldn't be swamped if you were both working down there!"

She felt a headache building up. It might be the combination of sore muscles from a crap ton of sewing, the suppression of her low-grade rage at Billy's whining and needling... or her worry for Jericho. The guy who had come up and into her apartment — Trevor? — seemed like bad news.

"You know, I never really asked about the guys Jericho hangs out with," Kyla said to Billy. "You've met them, haven't you?"

Billy shrugged. "Some of them. We hung out in Vegas. They seemed cool." He grinned, obviously remembering something. "Couple of 'em were crazy. Stayed out all night with a few of them. Of course, this was before I got with Lindsay."

Well, that didn't sound promising, she thought with a grimace. "Are they... I mean... What kind of crazy are we talking about?"

"They're not like Hell's Angels or anything," Billy said, catching her drift. "I'm sure a lot of them don't necessarily walk the straight and narrow, legally speaking, but it's not like they're out there killing people and running guns and stuff." He paused. "I don't think."

Definitely not promising. "But Jericho isn't involved in that stuff," she said, confident of that at least.

"Of course not." Billy scoffed. "For Jericho, it's always been about the bikes. You know that. He could take apart, build, and improve anything on two, three, or four wheels. Hell, he could probably build an eighteen-wheeler from scratch if he really wanted to, but it's the bikes themselves that he loves first. That and travelling."

She nodded. She knew how that felt... not necessarily for bikes but for the costumes. She wondered if Jericho might be able to fabricate some stuff for a Fallout 4 suit she had in mind, or possibly some armor. Hmmm.

"He's a big guy. Literally. He can take care of himself," Billy muttered. "He's not a puppy, and he's not the kid who used to crash on our floor."

"I know that," she answered back, snapping out of her costuming reverie.

"He's not staying," Billy added. "And when he goes, I'm gonna need you back in the shop. It's important."

She felt her spine stiffen, and for a quick second, she wanted to slap her brother. No, *punch* him. "Have I ever slacked, Billy? *Ever?*" She was unable to keep the tone of outrage out of her voice, and realized she didn't want to. Why should she play nice? He was the one being the butthead here!

Billy let out a breath, rubbing at his temple with his good hand. "No. I know that. You are really the engine that keeps Summers Auto running. No pun intended."

She felt slightly mollified. It seemed so rare that Billy recognized that.

"And I know you like this stuff. Hell, I like snowboarding and trying every steakhouse in North America as humanly possible," he said, and she found herself grinning a little. "But it's just a vacation, you know? I get how much you love this costume stuff, but Dad gave the shop to us, and it's our responsibility. Jericho is a crutch right now, but he's gonna go. And then it'll be you and me, making this work again." He sighed. "Besides, don't you want to show him how well you can manage this? Do you want him to think you're too weak to pull it together on your own?"

Before she could splutter an angry response to this, Billy held up his hand.

"Just... think about it." He disappeared down the stairs.

Furious, she went back to sewing, finishing up the Liliana costume with jabbing thrusts of the needle for the touch-up work. She just had to get the Daenerys costume together, she mentally crossed off. She would probably need to call the contest coordinator to get the exact details. The link that Cressida had sent her went to a website that was down, although she'd gotten the details from Reddit and the notes Cressida had taken. Just one more thing, she thought. Billy expected her to keep working in the shop, she still had one costume to finish up, and now this...

She was growling to herself when Jericho stomped up. "Here's your shake," he said, handing it to her.

He was obviously in a foul mood if that scowl was anything to go by. Her initial instinct was to lash back, but her previous worry reigned, and she bit back a sharp reply, getting to her feet and putting the shake on a nearby table. "What happened? What's wrong?"

"Nothing." His face was stern.

She stood, moving to him. "Not nothing," she pressed. "It was those guys, wasn't it? The guys from your, um, motorcycle club?"

He spun. "We're *not* a motorcycle club!"

She wasn't sure why that particular description would be so offensive. "Um... okay. Your crew? Collective? The men you ride around with?"

He grimaced, and she saw the muscles work on the side of his chiseled jaw. "Yeah. They are guys I sometimes ride with."

"What did they want?"

"I don't want to talk about it."

"Oh. All right." It felt like a rebuke, and she felt the sting of it. She knew she was already pissed at Billy, she reined in her own temper, projecting a bright smile. "Well, if you do decide to... I'm here."

"Thanks." But he still looked troubled, a mix of anger and frustration and a shot of something she couldn't describe.

She swallowed hard. She couldn't use offensive cheer on Jericho. She genuinely cared about him. "You know, if you're in any kind of trouble or anything, I'm always here."

She'd meant it as a balm. He'd been good about being her shoulder, and right now he was her downright salvation when it came to helping her out at the shop. But apparently this also hit some kind of hot button. His eyes narrowed. "What do mean, trouble?"

"You know. In a jam."

"What the hell do you think I'm mixed up in?" he said in a voice that could've frozen napalm. "Jesus, Kyla. What kind of thug do you think I am?"

"Okay, *overreaction*," she said, holding her hands up. "I just meant if you're in something messy with your friends, I'm happy to listen, and you know I'd do anything for you."

She paused, wondering how that sounded. And blushed a little. Actually, in normal circumstances, she'd love to do anything for him. And with him. Possibly to him.

She felt her cheeks blush.

"I ride with the Machinists. We're not a bunch of one percenter assholes, okay?" Jericho shouted.

"Well, I didn't think so," she said, confused. "Aren't they all millionaires or stockbrokers or something?"

That stopped him. "Wait, what?"

"You know. The one percent? Rich guys?" She made a peace sign. "Opposite of 'we are the ninety-nine percent' types?"

"No," he said, shaking his head. "I mean fucking criminal gangs on bikes. Bandidos, Hell's Angels, those guys. The ones the FBI goes after for criminal conspiracy, drug running, and murder."

"Okay." She took a deep breath. "Still not quite sure why you're yelling at me." She added some grit of her own to that statement. She'd put up with a lot, but yelling and cussing was crossing some lines, and she had her own anger ready to lash out.

"My mom was just like this, too," he said, and she realized what had happened. She'd tripped on a buried nerve. "Saying because I was hanging out with bikers that I was gonna turn into some kind of thug. *You're going to get in trouble. Why can't you just do the right thing?*" he growled. "Well, I'm not in any kind of trouble, I'm not in a jam, and I don't need your help!"

"Good, because if you keep raising your voice to me, you're certainly not going to get it," Kyla said with some heat of her own. "I care about you, Jericho. You have to know that. I just..."

He held up his hands. "I have to go out. I'm gonna take a ride."

She gritted her teeth, then nodded. "Sure. Take a house key if you want, be as late as you want. Or whatever."

He paused. Actually paused.

"Or, you know, you don't have to." *If you want to leave*, she thought. She steeled herself.

He grabbed the key with a grunt, then strode out, his long legs tearing up the space. He shut the door just short of a slam.

"Fine," she said to herself. "Just... fine."

"Hey, Kyla!" Billy shouted. "Jericho just left. You gonna come down and work on these cars?"

Peachy, she thought. Just... frickin'... peachy.

She didn't need kegels, she thought. She needed whiskey, stat.

· ♥ · ♥ · ♥ · ♥ · ♥ ·

That evening, Jericho leaned against a bar in Seattle. It was attached to a motorcycle parts shop, and it was a tiny biker bar, with classic motorcycles crowded out front. It had good beer on tap and only served peanuts and chips.

He felt almost immediately at home.

He needed this. He needed connection with his people. His...

Dammit, I'm not gonna say tribe.

It was getting near midnight. He'd ridden for a few hours, the best way he knew to clear his head. Then, when it hadn't helped, he'd decided to revisit his roots. Years ago, he'd originally met Pedro and some of the other Machinists in a tiny dive bar in Belltown. He'd hung out in the parking lot after being kicked out by the bartender, and he'd admired all the motorcycles as they rolled in. That was where he'd made his first big leap and found a group that understood him, accepted him. It didn't matter if he was white or Indian. All that mattered was how well he could handle a bike, and the quality of his work.

It was the most accepted he'd felt anywhere, before or since.

That bar had long since closed, turned into a Starbucks or something. This place had a similar vibe, at least. It was made up of gearheads, mechanics, and people who genuinely appreciated classics.

A willowy brunette walked up to him, leaning against the bar, batting her blue eyes at him. Her smile was broad. "You're new," she said, her voice low and husky.

He shrugged. "Not in town for long," he pointed out.

"Well, we'll just have to make the most of the time you're here," she purred. "Buy me a drink... What's your name?"

"Jericho." He gestured to the bartender, obliging him.

"Hello, Jericho." Her mouth curved. "I'm Kimber."

The girl reminded him of his last... well, he hesitated to say *girlfriend*, although he was very fond of her. Mellissa. He'd met her at a biker bar, too. She was built like this girl: thin as a rail, wearing crop tops and low-slung jeans over biker boots. He'd spent six months in Charlotte, doing custom work and getting his bike painted. He'd been with her for four of the six, and she'd been pissed when he told her it was time for him to leave. She'd expected him to stay.

She'd been cursing when he left.

Kimber tilted her hip as she leaned against the bar, angling her shoulder toward him. Her body language all but screamed invitation.

He sipped his now-warm beer and sighed. It had been a few months since he'd had sex, he realized, and she seemed on board with the temporary nature of his presence — it'd be a clear hookup.

"Nice T-shirt," Kimber said, stroking her long nails against the logo on his T-shirt. He waited for his body to feel something. She was pretty, he told himself gamely.

Unbidden, Kyla's moss-green eyes popped into his mind. Her smile.

Not helpful, he chastised himself.

"Who are the Machinists? Are they your MC?" Kimber asked, then tugged at the leather jacket he had resting on the barstool. "What are your colors?"

He flinched. "They're a group I hang with," he said, his words curt. "I don't ride with a motorcycle club."

"Huh. Okay." She rolled her eyes a little. "Just... you look like one of those guys, you know?"

"One of *what* guys?" He didn't mean to sound that defensive.

"You know," she said. "Jax. Tigs. Juice."

He blinked at her. What the hell was she talking about?

"Like the characters on that show... *Sons of Anarchy?*" she said, and then sighed impatiently. "It's only one of the best shows *ever*."

Oh, ugh. She was a biker groupie — and, based on her attitude, one whose fascination was based on the theoretical bad boys of a TV show. God help her if she ran into a *real* one-percenter crew. "You know, it's not really like that," he couldn't help but point out.

She laughed. "Well, it should be," she said. "Jax Teller is so hot and so badass! He's totally my spirit animal."

No, he fucking isn't. Because unless she was from a tribe, she didn't *have* a fucking spirit animal. And if she did, it wouldn't be some asshole playing a biker — from an outlaw motorcycle club, at that.

Jericho felt suddenly exhausted.

"You know that guy is British?" a new, male voice chimed in.

Jericho looked at the new arrivals like a lifeline while Kimber frowned, puzzled.

"Jax Teller is played by a Brit. He was made famous by his appearance on their version of *Queer as Folk.* He also auditioned for Thor and Anakin Skywalker but didn't get them."

Jericho stared at the man, startled. He was average height, maybe five ten, with bleached-white hair and tanned skin. He looked at least part Asian... Japanese, maybe?

"Also," he continued, "did you know that Ron Perlman was afraid of riding his bike in the first few episodes?"

Kimber's eyes narrowed at the man, not sure if he was making fun of her or what. Jericho suppressed his own smile.

Another taller man stood beside him, with close-cropped black hair and dark skin. Jericho was surprised — he looked Native American. He found himself wondering what tribe. "Dude," the man said, nudging his friend, "you know too much weird shit."

"True, but I'm always right," the bleached-haired guy agreed, then turned his attention to Jericho. "You the one driving that Norton Commando?"

Jericho nodded.

"Sweet ride," he said, then held out a hand. "I'm Tadashi. This is Mark."

"Jericho," he said, shaking, then introduced Kimber, who was sulking even while she sized up the new arrivals. She sipped at her beer.

"So, new around here? Don't remember seeing you," he said to Jericho.

"Just in town for a few weeks," Jericho replied.

"In Seattle?"

"Eastside," he said. "Snoqualmie."

Mark's expression turned curious. "You from the tribe?"

Surprised, Jericho nodded.

"Like the casino?" Kimber piped up. "Maybe you could take me there. I hear they've got a hotel, too." She did everything but wiggle her eyebrows at him and wink.

Jericho sighed. "I'm staying with a girl," he said gently but firmly.

"Like, a friend?" she said, with a slightly naughty smile.

"Well, I'm sleeping in her bed, so I'd say we're pretty friendly."

She flinched. Then she huffed, flouncing off to another group of guys. One wore colors, Jericho noted, and worried.

Mark laughed silently. "She was here last week, too," he said. "I get the feeling she's just broken up with some guy, and she's looking for a rebound or something, with a total badass biker. Walk on the wild side, that kinda shit."

Jericho shook his head. "I'm not looking to be anybody's summer slumming," he said sourly. "Still, she seems like she might get in over her head."

"Don't worry," Tadashi assured him. "The people who hang out here are cool. Angie, the bartender, keeps an eye out, and nobody's going to let her get in over her head without at least saying something."

Jericho glanced at his watch. "I ought to get going. I've got work in the morning." Probably a backlog of it — since he'd basically walked out after snarling at Kyla that afternoon.

He would have to apologize, he realized. That had been a dick move.

"At least show me your bike before you go?" Tadashi said, his expression eager.

Jericho nodded, and they followed him out. Tadashi let out a low whistle. "Factory original or custom?"

"I swapped out the Amals with modern carbs," Jericho said. "Updated the wiring looms, added disc brakes."

"This paint job is sick," Tadashi said, getting in close to stare. "Never seen anything like it."

Jericho couldn't help but puff out with pride. "Friend of mine in North Carolina did it for me. Took three tries, but we finally got it the way I wanted."

"What *is* it?" Tadashi asked.

He frowned. "It isn't anything, really. I just wanted it sorta dark blue on the top, then fading down to that silver."

"Not metal flake, though," Tadashi said, running his finger along the side. "What are these? Like, triangles?"

"Not exactly."

Mark, who had been studying the bike silently, suddenly laughed. "That's a *skʷəxʷic*, dude."

Jericho blinked. It'd been so long since he'd heard Lushootseed spoken that it felt like a shock. Even more of a shock — he recognized it, even if he didn't remember the word precisely.

Seeing Jericho's surprised expression, Mark shook his head. "Silver salmon," he translated, then pointed to the gradation of blue to green to grayish-silver, the flecks and hints of fish scale. "You painted your bike like a fucking silver salmon, dipshit."

Jericho stared at his bike as if he'd never seen it before. Now that the guy pointed it out ... it was beyond obvious.

It *was* just like a silver salmon.

Mark was still laughing at him. "You can take a kid out of the river, but you can't take the river out of the kid, yeah?"

Jericho felt shaken. "You from the tribe?"

"Dxʷlilap," Mark corrected. "You know, Tulalip. Grew up on the rez."

"You been here all this time?" Jericho asked.

Mark laughed harder. "Hell no," he said. "Tried Los Angeles for a while. Jesus, that place is a pit."

Jericho grinned. "Depends on where."

"Not for me, thanks," Mark said. "I don't mind visiting other places, but this is home."

Jericho sighed. He didn't know what that felt like... not really. But apparently living here had left more of an impression on him than he'd thought.

CHAPTER 6

He hung out with Tadashi and Mark longer than he expected, so Jericho rolled his motorcycle up to Kyla's building at around one in the morning. He wondered if she was still up and working. Of course, if he hadn't ditched her after lunch, she might have been able to have gotten more work done, he thought. He wondered if he had upset her.

   He let himself in with the key she'd given him. The light was still on in her workroom. "Kyla?" he said softly, taking off his boots at the door with some effort. Then he strode over to the spare room.

   She had left the light on, but she wasn't there. He did notice she'd gotten a lot of work done on the latest project. The dress thing he'd seen yesterday had been more pieces stuck to that dummy torso than an actual piece of clothing, but now it looked all sewn together, with different bits of embroidery or whatever. It looked like something people would pay a lot of money for. She must've worked like a demon to get that accomplished. He wondered how she was able to keep going, flawlessly, fearlessly, even when shit like her brother's arm came up.

She was amazing.

He'd never realized it until he'd left.

He turned off the light, then headed to the bedroom. "Kyla?"

She was dressed in her usual: a pair of boy-shorts and a loose T-shirt, this time with what looked like the Punisher logo on it. She'd left the curtain open a little, letting some moonlight through, and his eyes adjusted to the dimness. She'd kicked off most of the blankets. She was all luscious curves, he couldn't help but notice. Large, sumptuous breasts that curved into her generous waist before flaring out into hips that a guy could really dig his fingers into.

And, God help him... that ass. *Dayum.* He didn't consider himself particularly fascinated with that attribute before, but he found himself drawn to it on her.

The girl at the bar had provoked nothing in him but irritation and a bit of concern. Now, his body was tightening with a whole different kind of frustration.

Again: this is Kyla, you asshole. Get it together.

The thought was like a towel snapped across his balls, and he winced. Yeah, she wasn't some biker mama, looking for a good time. He needed to lock that shit down.

"You awake?" he said, ignoring the throb of his body, trying to get himself into line.

She rustled a little. "Yeah," she finally admitted. "You still mad?"

"No." He took a deep breath, then stretched out next to her. "I'm sorry, Kyla. I was a dick."

"Yeah, you kinda were," she agreed, and he laughed. "So, what was really going on? Because I get the feeling that wasn't about me."

He let out a deep breath. "I'm not used to talking to people about this."

"Of course you're not," she said. "You have testicles."

"That's sexist," he shot back, laughing. "Anyway, the Machinists have been my family since my Mom kicked me out. They got me. They supported me. They were the people I belonged with. I hadn't felt anything like that since you guys."

"Oh, Jericho." She curled up against him, and he instinctively put his arm out so she was cradled in a horizontal hug. She stroked the side of his face. "I'm so sorry, sweetie. But you know you could've stayed with us."

"And done what?" Jericho said, trying not to be distracted by the feel of her fingertips on his jawline. "I wanted to ride and see things and build things. Your father said I couldn't work at the shop unless I finished school, and I already knew that wasn't what I wanted. And with my Mom kicking me out... I'd already spent enough time on Billy's floor or on your couch or an air mattress. I wanted to start living my own life, not on your family's charity."

"It wasn't charity," Kyla said. It was amazing how that soft jade color of her eyes could snap in the pale moonlight. "We love you."

"I get that. Now, anyway," he admitted. "But the Machinists were the right choice for me then. Now, they're growing and changing. There's a lot of turmoil. I want to help the younger guys, the newer guys, the way they helped me. And I don't want to see things go wrong."

She was quiet. "You want to make sure they're safe, like your friends helped you," she said softly.

"Yeah. Maybe."

"You're a good man, Jericho Salomon."

He smiled ruefully. "Sure I am. But don't tell anybody. I've got a rep to think of."

She smiled, then nuzzled his chest with her forehead. "Don't yell at me again, though," she said. "Because I didn't like it."

"I'm sorry, babe. I won't do it again."

"And I'll hurt you," she added.

He burst out laughing, hugging her. "You are *fierce*, you know that?"

They stayed like that for a long moment, arms around each other, stretched out against each other. He could get used to this, he realized. He took a breath, inhaling the smell of her hair. Her bright scent, her comforting warmth, cast a spell on him. It was like being seduced into napping by late summer sunshine.

He shifted a little, rubbing his lips on the top of her head, pressing a few kisses here and there. She made a happy humming noise.

She was still in his arms. Her hand was on his chest. He shifted a tiny bit, pulling her a little tighter to him, and she curved easily against him. Unfortunately, that pressed her amazing breasts against his chest, and he felt his stomach tighten — among other things.

He rubbed his fingertips along her back, stroking the thin T-shirt fabric. Her hum went a little lower, a touch more growly. He could feel the fleeting brush of her lips against his chest, although he couldn't be sure. Maybe it was just an accident. Maybe it was all in his head.

What would it be like to kiss her?

She shifted again, a restless motion, bringing her hips closer to the crotch of his jeans.

It was like lighting a fuse. His cock started to stretch towards her. It was like his entire body was iron, and she was a magnet drawing him inexorably closer to her.

"Jericho," she sighed.

Touch her, his body screamed. *Kiss her.*

Take her.

He blinked, shaking himself out of the sex-coma he'd started to fall under.

Take her? What the fuck?

He disengaged like he'd found a rattler in the bed, causing her to yelp. "What? What is it?"

"I need to take a shower," he blurted out. "Before I go to sleep. Don't want to get your bed all dirty."

"Oh," she said, sounding disoriented. "Okay."

"Get some sleep. Good night," he said, and ran for the bathroom. Turning the water on cold, he jumped in.

Get it together, he mentally chastised his cock. *Nobody is "taking" anybody anywhere. Especially not Kyla frickin' Summers.*

Kyla decided she needed to stop fantasizing about Jericho. That was all there was to it.

Last night, after he'd gotten back, he'd apologized, and they'd snuggled it out. It felt like it had been ages since she'd snuggled with anyone. Her past boyfriends hadn't really been big snugglers. Into sex, hell yeah, but the aftermath was not really companionable. Since she was "one of the guys" in so many ways, they figured she'd be "tough" enough to avoid the touchy-feely side of a relationship. They'd go back to watching football or playing video games or just roll over and start snoozing. Kyla had grown up a tomboy, and that this hadn't bothered her for a long time. Now that she was indulging more of her "girly" side with the cosplay, she realized that she didn't have to be quite so rigid in her gender interpretation. She could like wielding a sword and enjoying a good grapefruit-scented bath bomb. She could wear high heels or hiking boots. As her friend Mallory would say, women weren't just binary — you didn't have to be one thing or another.

Too bad she couldn't say the same about her relationship with Jericho.

You can be his friend. That's pretty much the only option there.

That said, there was a moment where she could've sworn she'd felt and heard his heartbeat speed up beneath her cheek. His muscles had flexed beneath her palm. She sneaked the teeniest, tiniest kiss on his chest. Then maybe, just maybe, plastered herself against him.

Then he'd leaped out of bed like his hair was on fire, insisting he had to take a shower that second.

She prayed that she hadn't made him uncomfortable. Of course, she'd listened to him take a long shower (and, *yeeeeah*, fantasized a hell of a lot about what *that* might look like), then he'd climbed in, said a quick "g'night," and started sleeping with his back to her. Although honestly, he'd still seemed kind of tense, and the way he was breathing sounded like he might've been faking it.

Of course, she'd been exhausted, so she'd gotten to sleep not too long after that, but it did puzzle her... until she remembered. He probably didn't want her getting ideas. He had to know about her crush on him when she was younger, and there she was, draped over him like a poncho. It was probably his gentle way of giving them some distance.

She sighed. She really, really needed to get better about that. It was unfair to him, and painful for her. They could joke like always, but she had to keep her hormones on lockdown before anything else bad happened.

By late morning, she stretched and then did a full-on dance in her living room. "*Woot!*" she shouted, shuffling and swinging, doing the Sprinkler and the Washing Machine and every other dorktastic dance she could think of. "Who's the sewing boss? *I am the fucking sewing boss!*"

She had finished up the costumes. She had Liliana done, complete with props. She had Megara finished. The wigs were styled. She was going to do the finishing touches on the Daenerys dress, but damn it, she was *finished*. It had been a push, but with Jericho's help at the shop, it was all coming together with time to spare. She could finally breathe easily.

She just needed to follow up with the contest coordinators to make sure that *Game of Thrones* counted since it was both a book and a TV show, and the parameters she'd gotten were unclear. She'd already sent a few emails that hadn't gotten returned, so she decided to call. She might be able to get a bead on what other people were going to bring, too. She couldn't ask about previous winners or anything, but it couldn't hurt.

"Hello?" a voice said on the other line, sounding harried. "Custom Cosplay Creations Catalogs."

"Hi, this is Kyla Summers," Kyla said. "I left a message and some emails. I'm going to be at this month's OtakuCon, and I wanted to double-check some of the conditions of the contest?"

"The contest? Oh, right, the contest. Sorry. We're processing the photos from the other contests."

"Other contests?" she repeated, feeling numb. "What other contests?"

"This isn't just local to the PNW," the man clarified. "We've got contests in Tampa, San Diego, Boston, and Minneapolis, as well."

Kyla froze. Oh, shit. She hadn't realized she was competing on that level.

"OtakuCon is going to be our last one," he said. "There will be a ten-thousand-dollar reward for each one locally, of course, but the contest and the *Entertainment Weekly* spot will go to the grand prize winner judged over all of them."

Oh, shit. Oh, shit. She felt her palms go sweaty. "I'm, um, entering a Megara, a Liliana from *Magic: The Gathering* — the card game — and, um, a Daenerys Stormborn. From the show, although I guess it could be from the book." She cleared her throat. "I wanted to make sure that was, um, okay? Using a tabletop card game instead of a video game?"

Or am I just going to be crushed? She felt her heart sink.

"I like that! We don't see stuff like that enough. I don't think any of the previous winners have something like that, actually," he said, and she cheered up a bit. "I think having a video game character in that would help a lot. What about your male characters?"

Her mind went blank. "My... what?"

"Three female characters, three male characters," he said, as if he hadn't just dropped a bomb on her whole game plan. "And one of the male-female pairings is a couple. Did you not get the official rules?"

"I got what was posted on a wiki, from the original site. It was an email."

"Oh. We updated that ages ago," he said. "Didn't you check the website... Oh, right. That's been down." He sounded embarrassed. "I'm sorry."

"No problem," she heard herself say hollowly. "Thanks for your time."

She hung up, then sunk down on the living room floor, hugging her knees.

Three male costumes. At least one based on a video game.

How the hell was she supposed to pull that off?

Jericho opened the door. "So what's all the stomping about? Heard you were celebrating... What happened?" he said, sinking down next to her. "Are you hurt? What is it?"

"I talked to the contest coordinators," she said, and tears started streaming down her face. "I was supposed to do three male costumes, too. I didn't know."

"That's bad, huh?"

"I don't have them!" she said on a sob. "I don't have time to make them! I don't... God, Jericho. How am I supposed to do this? And I dragged you all this way, and now it's all pointless!"

"Bullshit," he said, and he pulled her up on his lap. "It's not pointless. You worked your ass off. You always do. And I volunteered to come here, remember? It's not like you had a gun to my head."

She made a raspberry noise at this.

He stroked her cheek, nudging her so that she was forced to look at him. His expression was fierce. "I care about you, Kyla. You get that, right? I want to help you. This isn't pity or because you're a family friend. You are one of my favorite people. You are hardworking and loyal and amazing."

She smiled, wiping away the tears and stemming the flow. "Right. My work ethic brings all the boys to the yard."

He laughed. "I was going to say this rockin' bod, but you do have a smokin' ethic there."

She leaned against him. "I just... I really, really wanted to win this," she said softly. "Not just because of the contest. Because... because of the dream behind it, you know? I wanted this. I wanted to prove that this wasn't some stupid dream. I wanted to go for something that I wanted, without justifying it to anyone."

"Nobody says you can't," he said. When she shrugged, he jiggled her. "Seriously. I know you. If you want something, you will move fucking heaven and hell to get it."

"For my friends, maybe. For my family, definitely." She sniffed. "Not so much for myself."

Now he stood on his feet and looked her dead in the eye.

"Well, you do it for me, then," he said. "Because you deserve this. Got me? And I know if I wanted this, you'd probably be mainlining coffee and... I don't know, holding people at gunpoint and forcing them to help me so I could win."

She let out a snort. "That's probably true, actually."

"So do it for *you* this time. All right?"

She took a deep, shaky breath. "Okay."

He nodded. "Good."

He moved in to give her a hug, she thought. Maybe a kiss on the cheek for comfort and encouragement.

Problem was, she was thinking of giving him a kiss on the cheek for thanks, and they both turned the wrong way. Or, as their lips connected, the right one.

They stood frozen for a second, lips pressed gently against each other, stunned.

Then she closed her eyes. *I'm just gonna enjoy this for a second*, she reasoned.

Apparently her body heard "enjoy" and interpreted it as "dive head first" which it then promptly proceeded to do.

She clutched her fingers into his T-shirt, pulling him down to meet her now ravenous lips. She let out a low sound, surprise mixed with desire, and parted her lips. She probably meant to take a breath. Her tongue swiping out to slick against his lower lip was probably just an accident.

Probably.

You should stop, she told herself, even as she got up on her toes, pressing her body to his.

Then, in a blink, he held her tight against him, curving her to him, his mouth moving. And she realized with shock that she might not be the only one enjoying this.

God, his *kisses*.

He opened his mouth, his tongue tangling with hers, stroking it, long and strong and *oh my God* talented. She shuddered against him. He twined his fingers in her hair, holding her face to his as his other hand moved down, cupping her ass, squeezing it, pulling her tighter to him and...

Her eyes flew open. He was hard, and getting harder. Her nipples stuck out like antennae, and she couldn't suppress a moan.

He pulled back long enough to groan himself. "Kyla," he breathed.

She pulled at his shoulders, dragging him back to her. They were all over each other, breathing raggedly. He nipped down her throat, licking her collarbone. She bit his earlobe, reveling in his crazed growl of pleasure.

"Bedroom," she said, out of her mind. "Now."

The words seemed to drag him back to sanity. He tore himself away, blinking. "Wait. What?"

His sanity, in turn, spurred hers. "Sorry?"

"You said... you want to..."

"Huh? I just... I said..." She cleared her throat. "Bathroom. I... um, have to go to the bathroom. Now."

He blinked again slowly, like he'd been clubbed with a crescent wrench.

"So, okay!" She slapped on her mega-bright smile. "Thanks!"

She fled, locking the door, rubbing her hands over her face, then mouthed to herself in the mirror: *Thanks?*

What the hell was she thinking?

"Do you, um, want some lunch? I can pick up some lunch," Jericho said through the door.

"Lunch!" She grabbed it like a lifeline. "Yes! That sounds perfect!"

"Right. I'm gonna... grab... some lunch."

She heard him leave, closing the door behind him. Then she splashed water on her face, feeling like the biggest idiot *ever*.

· ♥ · ♥ · ♥ · ♥ · ♥ ·

Don't think about it. Do not think about it.

He and Kyla had just... No. He wasn't going to think about it. Because if he thought about it, then he'd think about her reaction to it. And his body's *continued* reaction to it.

So he wasn't going to think about it.

Denial is a hell of a drug.

He decided to go over to the Black Dog Café to pick up some sandwiches. Kyla had a T-shirt from there, so he figured she liked the food.

And you want to make Kyla happy, don't you?

"Still not thinking about it," he muttered, forcing himself to focus instead on the town. He'd driven past the casino on the way in. It had been on the cusp of opening when he'd left, and he hadn't paid much attention to it. Now, there was a convenience store and gas station next to it.

It was weird to see how much things had changed since he'd left. He'd gone the summer before the casino had opened, for example, which was right up the hill from Herfy's. It was a huge, gorgeous, monolithic thing, or at least what he'd seen had been. He imagined his mother and grandmother either loved the thing or hated it. He wondered what his uncle thought about it. They'd all been proud of their heritage as S'duxalbix, the real name of the Snoqualmie tribe. Still, the idea of slot machines and blackjack tables wasn't a part of the stories his grandmother used to tell him. He felt disoriented by it, out of place. Not that he'd ever felt like he'd fit in, but... it was like a car, he thought. An old car he hadn't been fond of, but now was completely refurbished, and he wasn't sure how he felt about it or how it handled. So much was changing. So many things that he'd taken for granted, that were suddenly unexpected and exciting and completely changed.

Still. Not. Thinking. About. It.

He walked into the eclectic cafe. Some kind of indie-bohemian quasi-country music was playing, and he was glad he'd missed the lunch rush since it was almost one o'clock. He placed his order for sandwiches and sat at a table to wait, studying the paintings and photographs on the walls around him.

A poster said Thomas the Train was going to be there that weekend, at the historic train depot. He could see the blue locomotive engine, with what he assumed was its "face" on the front covered with a canvas. He shook his head. The town sure had changed.

A flash of his kiss with Kyla popped up, unbidden.

For God's sake, put a leash on it!

He gritted his teeth, wishing that something, anything, would drive the images and lush sensations and sheer desire from his mind.

He heard the squeak of the front door opening behind him. "Hey there, Linda," a man's voice called to the waitress behind the counter, who smiled back.

"Hey, Gary," she said.

He froze. He recognized the voice. Knew the name.

He turned, slowly, feeling his stomach form into a ball of ice.

It was Gary, his stepfather.

They'd known each other all of four years before Jericho had struck out on his own. Gary had started dating his mother when he was fourteen, moved in the following year, and they'd married shortly thereafter. Unlike the town, Gary hadn't changed too much. He was medium height, maybe five ten or so. Still wore a button-down and khakis like he was born in business casual. his black hair was shot through with a bit of gray now, at the temples, and his skin was slightly more wrinkled, more laugh lines around his dark brown eyes. His reddish-brown skin was a little paler than Jericho's, probably because Jericho spent more time riding around with the sun on his face. Jericho wondered if that meant Gary had been trapped in the office more, and if he still worked at Microsoft.

This is not how I wanted to be distracted, Jericho thought.

"Jericho," Gary said, quiet shock in his voice.

"Hey, Gary." Jericho was amazed his voice was as calm as it was. His heart seemed to pound in his chest like an over-revving engine.

Gary's mouth worked, as if he was trying out words but couldn't find the right ones. Finally he walked over, hand out. Jericho instinctively went to shake, but Gary pulled him in for a hug. "How are you? When did you get in?" Gary said, pounding him on the back and holding tight.

Now it was Jericho's moment to be speechless. He took a step back, shoving his hands in his pockets. He cleared the sudden hoarseness in his throat. "I've only been here a little while," he finally croaked. "Helping out some friends."

"Oh?" Gary's face fell. "Well, you wouldn't have known how to reach us, anyway." Then he winced.

Because you don't know how to contact us, and we didn't know how to contact you. And it's been nine years. Gary didn't say it and didn't have to. It was obvious.

Jericho felt every muscle in his back tense, his spine going straight. God, this was awkward. Because he knew damned well he hadn't planned on looking for them. That said, now that he'd seen him...

"How have you been?" he asked. A safe, neutral question.

"Busy," Gary said with a small laugh. "Still working at Microsoft. Updates never sleep. And you?" He looked at Jericho carefully, his eyes lingering on the Machinists T-shirt. "Still, um... riding your motorcycle?"

Still a part of a gang, you mean? The question hovered there, understood if not spoken.

Jericho sighed. "Yeah. Still doing that."

"Okay. That's... okay."

They stood there, awkwardly for a moment. Jericho chafed under the silence. "How's Mom?"

"Oh, exhausted and crazed," Gary said with a laugh, causing Jericho's eyes to widen. He hadn't expected Gary to be quite that honest. "But that's par for the— Oh." He stopped himself. "You don't know."

Suddenly, Jericho felt his whole body constrict with panic. "What? Is she sick? Hurt? Is she all right?"

So much had changed in Snoqualmie, he realized. But he'd never thought of his mother being anything other than her usual bossy, angry, judgmental self. But still there. Still healthy. Still the same.

"She's all right," Gary reassured him quickly. "She's just... I mean, we're... She..."

The door opened again. "Gary, help me, would you?" his mother said, tugging at a young child who was crying. "He wants to see Thomas, but I told him not till this—"

She stopped short, her mouth dropping open as she stared.

Jericho felt his heart clutch. She had changed. She'd put on weight. That wasn't a bad thing — he remembered that she'd been skinny, and weary, most of his life. The extra pounds had softened her, made her face look less drawn... less anxious. Her hair was still jet-black, with the slightest wave, and it still hung long, almost to her waist. She wore it in a long ponytail. She was wearing a blouse that said Snoqualmie Casino and a pair of worn jeans, as well as a broken-in pair of moccasins. She did look tired, but she looked more shocked.

"Jericho?" she breathed, her dark eyes going wide as the moon.

He stared down at the wailing child, whose hand she was holding. He had dark brown eyes, jet-black hair. The clear skin dark no doubt from running around in the sun.

It was like looking at a picture of himself from childhood, only darker. The kid had his mother's eyes, the strong chin and high cheekbones they both shared.

He stared at the kid.

The kid seemed to notice, his wailing winding down as he investigated this new person. With a sudden burst of shyness, he quickly hid behind his mother.

Their mother, Jericho realized.

"Here are your sandwiches," the waitress said, oblivious to the drama happening in front of her.

"Jericho..." Gary said, putting a hand on his arm. "Meet Sam. Your brother."

My brother.

He had a brother.

His head swam.

His mother's eyes filled. "Jericho..."

He couldn't deal with this. Not right now. "Hi, Mom."

"You're... you're back?"

He nodded, unable to speak.

"For good?"

"A visit," he said. "Just helping some friends."

He didn't mean to sound that curt. But damn it, he wasn't prepared for this.

She looked down at the floor as Sam fussed behind her legs. She pulled the kid up, resting him on her hip. "I..." She blinked, tears resting on her lashes. "It's good to see you."

He nodded.

"Maybe..." She took a deep breath. "Maybe... we could see you? Talk a bit?"

He nodded. He felt like he was drowning with emotions he couldn't handle.

"Where are you staying?"

"I'm helping out the Summers," he said. "Billy and Kyla."

"The ones with the auto shop?" she asked, a note of surprise in her voice. "You stayed in touch with them?"

He heard the judgment, the hurt, and his jaw tightened.

"Yes," he said, his response sharp. "I did."

She winced, as if he'd slapped her. He felt guilt puddling up with resentment.

He had to get out of here. *Now*.

"Here," Gary said, pressing a business card in his hand. "My cell's on there, and... um, our address. Why don't you give us a call? We'll be able to set up something. A dinner, maybe. I'm sure your uncle and grandmother would love to see you, too."

Jericho nodded uncomfortably. "I... have to go. Gotta bring lunch," he said, holding up the bag.

His mother's face fell. "All right," she said softly.

He didn't hug them. Just nodded again, feeling like an asshole, and strode out, sweating, anxiety boiling through him.

What the hell had just happened?

And what the hell was he supposed to do next?

On the plus side, he thought with gallows humor, *at least you're not worried about the Kyla issue anymore.*

CHAPTER 7

Kyla wasn't proud. When Jericho said he was going to grab some lunch, she'd fled like a thief, telling Billy to tell Jericho she'd just remembered she had to do something. That "something" was panic-calling one of her best friends, Mallory Price, and asking to see her ASAP. A quick drive to Bellevue had them meeting at a phở restaurant. Thankfully, Mallory was waiting for her.

"Who'd you kill?" Mallory said without preamble.

"Nobody yet," Kyla replied, locking her car. "But after my total embarrassment today, might be me before the day's over."

"Embarrassment, huh? I was expecting a bit more of an emergency, honestly. Not that I mind, but why didn't you just hit up Cressida or Hailey down at Fandoms? Why come all this way?"

Kyla bit her lip, hedging, as they walked in and sat at a table. Mallory was definitely the least stereotypically "girly" friend Kyla had, and she prided herself on being the most logical, least romantic. She identified as gender fluid and liked to break stereotypes where she could — not as a rebellion thing, simply as a... well, a Mallory thing. Today, she looked sharp as a razor, her lean figure showcasing a pair of black slacks, a white button-up shirt with French cuffs, the throat open and a loose-tugged midnight-blue tie that matched her eyes. She topped it all with a black vest with a pocket watch — a damned pocket watch. Her toffee-colored hair was cut short, artfully put up in some kind of spiky 'do.

"You always look so pulled together," Kyla said ruefully, glancing down at her own jeans and Rainbow Dash T-shirt with the slogan 20% cooler than you. "Like a cross between the Thin White Duke and Spike from *Cowboy Bebop*. We are polar opposites."

"You are the sunshine to my dark side, the Hufflepuff to my Slytherin," Mallory agreed. "The elusive creative genius to my doggedly tenacious legal mind. Which is telling me, by the way, that you are stalling. Spill. What happened that had you calling me in a panic?"

Kyla swallowed hard, then glanced around — as if anybody here actually cared what she was talking about. "I've been sleeping with Jericho."

Mallory grinned, turning over her Vietnamese coffee, letting it drip into the evaporated milk. "Jericho Salomon? Huge, biker badass type? *That* Jericho?" she clarified, then unleashed a wicked grin. "Well done, you!"

"Wait. Not that kind of sleeping with," Kyla said quickly.

Mallory wadded up a napkin and tossed it at her. "Awww. Hiss, boo."

"We've been *sharing a bed*," Kyla said. "Long story why. Anyway, today, he was hugging me because I had a bad morning and I was crying, and then we were laughing, and then... I kissed him. Or he kissed me." She huffed. "We *kissed*."

Mallory studied her while stirring her coffee, then took a sip. "Ahhhhh, caffeine." Her eyebrow quirked upward in a perfect arc. "Still not seeing the emergency here. What happened after that?"

"I tried to tell him we needed to go to the bedroom."

Mallory's eyes widened. "Must've been some kiss."

Kyla felt her whole body shiver. "Yeah."

"And his response to this was...?"

Kyla frowned. "He looked like I'd punched him in the face."

"I see. This is going south quickly." Mallory sighed. "He wasn't amenable to the idea, then?"

"I didn't hang around to find out," Kyla said, rubbing her face with her hands. "He asked what I'd said, and I told him I hadn't said bedroom, I'd said *bathroom*..."

Mallory burst out laughing, loud enough for other patrons to start staring at them.

"Shut up! Anyway, he said he was going to grab some lunch, and I fled and called you and here I am." She rested her head on the table. "Oh, God. What am I gonna do? How am I gonna face him?"

Kyla put her head down on the table, banging it lightly. After a second, she lifted her head to see the waitress looking at her with concern, bearing two huge bowls of phở and a plate of imperial rolls.

"She's fine, Thuy," Mallory reassured the waitress, winking at her. "Man troubles."

Thuy nodded knowingly, winking in response. "I've got booze in the back."

"We may get to that," Mallory said, then turned back to Kyla. "Okay. First things first," she said, breaking out a pair of chopsticks and mixing the meat with the noodles before dousing the whole thing with sriracha and dumping in jalapeños. "You kissed Jericho. What, exactly, are you afraid of? What's the worst thing that could happen?"

"It's a bad idea," Kyla hedged, picking up one of the crispy fried rolls and taking a pensive bite.

"Why, though?"

"Because I obviously wanted to take it further, and I don't think he did," Kyla said, poking at her beef and noodles.

"You sure about that?" Mallory challenged.

Kyla closed her eyes, thinking about the rigidity she'd started to feel against her stomach. "Well... maybe he was interested. On some level. But not as much as I was. And besides, he's here to *help* me. I asked for him to come out here. I took him away from the stuff he was doing in Las Vegas so he could take over in the shop while I make costumes. I didn't bring him out here just so I could jump him like a trampoline!"

"Still," Mallory laughed, "you can multitask, right?"

Kyla glared at her. "Not funny, Mallory."

"Not meant to be," Mallory replied, unoffended. "Let me play devil's advocate here."

"Shocker," Kyla muttered.

"Were you planning on coercing him to have sex with you? Bribing him? Physically forcing him?"

"What? No!"

Mallory leaned back a little in her chair, looking whip-lean and somewhat smug. "So you'll be offering him a proposition? One he will have complete autonomy to accept or refuse, correct?"

"Which he'll probably refuse," Kyla said, her stomach knotting. She pushed the egg roll away and started crumpling her paper napkin. "Or if he accepts, maybe it'll be because he feels sorry for me. Or because he's tired?"

"Or because you're a girl, and you're hot," Mallory added, eating her soup.

Kyla shook her head. "But if he says no, it'll be awkward. I'll have to hide."

"And if he says yes?"

Kyla thought about it for a second. Her brain really, really wanted to linger on that image. So did some other parts of her body. She shook her head, clearing it.

"I... I don't know. It seems like a bad idea. So much could go wrong."

"I see I'm going about this the wrong way." Mallory sighed. "Let's say you have sex with him, and it's terrible. Like semi-paralyzed-octopus-trying-to-play-billiards-with-a-spaghetti-noodle level of terrible."

Now it was Kyla's turn to laugh. Mallory shushed her. "Hey, weirder things have happened. Would you hate him?"

"No," Kyla said immediately.

"How do you know?" Mallory pressed.

"Because we'd be able to laugh it off. We'd be able to chalk it up to a bad experiment, and we'd still be friends," Kyla said, realizing that she had complete confidence in that answer. If it was a disaster, he wasn't the type who would blame her or hold a grudge. And even if she was a disaster, she certainly wasn't the type to blame or punish him, either. "I don't think I can bet on lousy sex to be the solution, though."

"Let's say it rocks your world," Mallory said, as if she was detailing a case. "And then he leaves, and you don't see him again for a few years. What's the worst that could happen?"

I could fall in love with him, she thought. Not a kid's crush this time. A woman who actually knew what she was missing.

"I could be miserable," Kyla finally answered.

"If I remember this right, with his baggage, he's gonna leave, sweetie," Mallory said gently. "Maybe he'll come back, but odds are good it's not to stay."

Kyla nodded glumly.

"It then seems to me that you have two choices. You have amazing, head-banging sex, with the full and clear understanding that it is *not* a relationship. Or you make the clear decision not to engage in any sex, period — great, horrible, or in between. Feel any better?"

Kyla thought about it. What if she was in control of the situation? Knowing that he wasn't going to stay? Because it was preposterous to think that he might. "That actually helps a little."

Mallory took a sip of coffee and sent her a knowing smile. "You're going to go for the head-banging, I take it."

Kyla felt her cheeks heat.

"Well, I've given my official counsel. What you do with it is up to you." Mallory grinned. "I will add, if you really want to guarantee the cutoff, tell him that you're scratching an itch. That you're obviously both attracted, but it's just as obvious that he's not going to stay, so you guys will bang like bunnies while he's here, and then when he leaves, you will speak of this to no one. Just a little temporary arrangement. An aberration. That puts you in the driver's seat, helps you compartmentalize, and keeps your heart from getting broken. Or at least, if it does get broken, it will limit the damage. He won't ask, because you were up-front. And you'll know that you made it clear from the jump, so you've got no one to blame but yourself."

Kyla stared at her. "You're good," she joked. "You should be a lawyer."

"Shoulda seen me when I was a D.A." Mallory answered with a wink. "That's why they pay me the big bucks, cupcake. Which reminds me... one last piece of advice?"

"Yeah?"

"Wear lingerie," Mallory said. "Gives you a better bargaining position."

Jericho glanced at the large clock on the wall of the shop. Six o'clock. He'd been working like a demon since he'd picked up lunch and run into his mother and stepfather.

And little brother. Don't forget that.

His mind was darting around like a trapped rat, scrabbling frantically. Of course, if the thought of his family left him confused and cold, his brain would then fixate on the other gnarly problem — his mind-blowing kiss with Kyla, earlier that day. Which made him confused and hot. Really, really hot.

Good thing he could fix cars on auto-pilot, because his brain was absolutely no fucking help today.

"Dude," Billy said, stepping out into the shop. "We can shut down for the night. You've got us caught up, and I promised Kyla no big jobs. We'll just be looking at brakes and mufflers and shit for the rest of the week. You've been working in Beast Mode."

Jericho smiled weakly. Ever since he and Kyla had their little "moment" that morning, he'd felt weirder than ever talking to Billy.

"You okay?"

Jericho let out a breath. "Ran into Gary this afternoon," he said, finally. "And Mom."

Billy's jaw dropped. "No shit. What happened?"

"It was fine. I only saw them for like a minute." Jericho rubbed at the back of his neck. "They have a kid."

"*No shit!*"

GAME OF HEARTS

Jericho let out a weak laugh. "He's like three. I have a brother. I didn't even know I had a brother."

"Why the fuck didn't they tell you?" Billy said, incensed. "It was bad enough that your mother kicked you out, but to just up and fucking have a kid and never tell you — what the hell? Is it like you don't even exist? What, they were starting over with one that might actually do what she tells it to?"

"Honestly, I thought the same thing this afternoon," Jericho agreed. "But the more I thought about it, the more I realized this is on me. I never got in contact with them. I never told them how to get in contact with me."

"Well, okay." Billy frowned. "But why should you? Your Mom was always pushing you. She never wanted you to be who you were. Hell, she kicked you out and said if you left you might as well have been dead. You weren't part of the family."

"True." And that still hurt.

"So fuck that. Fuck them." Billy was getting more worked up over it than he was.

"They gave me their number," Jericho responded slowly. "And said I should call. Like, maybe we should get together for dinner."

"Yeah? Well they can take their dinner invitation and shove..."

"Billy," Jericho stopped him. "I don't know. It's been nine years. I'm not the same guy I was."

"You're going to forgive them? Just like that?" Now Billy looked pissed. "Your Mom was never home..."

"She was working a lot," Jericho interjected.

"... and when she was, she was yelling at you all the time..."

"I was a teenage boy," Jericho pointed out. "Now that I run into motorhead kids in their teens, I don't know how she didn't strangle me some days."

Billy grimaced. "You fuckin' cried, dude. You stayed here because she was so mean."

Jericho looked away. He had forgotten that part. Mostly.

"I'm not saying what she did was right. And I don't regret leaving, not one fucking minute," Jericho said slowly.

Billy nodded, as if his point was proven.

"What I'm saying is, maybe I see if she has something to say."

Like *I'm sorry*. That might be worth hearing. It was probably a long shot though.

"And maybe I just can't keep being a pussy about Snoqualmie. Not dealing with this shit has kept me from seeing you and Ky for the past nine years. What is wrong with me that I couldn't even come back here because of some shit? This is my hometown, too, right?"

"Hell, yeah."

Jericho nodded. "So... yeah. I'll see." Strangely, he felt better. Which was weird, since Billy was many things, but touchy-feely was not one of them. Still, the conversation had helped him feel better about that whole situation than he'd felt in a long time.

"It would be nice to have you visit more," Billy said, itching absently at his cast. "Mom and Dad tend to come back for the summer, after the floods and before the snows, as Dad says. And God knows Kyla misses the hell out of you. She cried when you left."

Guilt slammed Jericho like a hammer. "It's been nice to see her," he said, as innocently as possible. His voice sounded like he was being strangled.

Fortunately, Billy wasn't terribly perceptive, either. "God, remember the crush she used to have on you?"

Jericho blinked. "Huh?"

"Oh, come on. You can't tell me you didn't notice." Billy started laughing. "She was always mooning about you. I think I caught her writing 'Jericho loves Kyla' with little hearts on her notebook all through middle school."

"That was a hell of a long time ago," Jericho said, his guilt shifting in another direction. He'd kissed her — they'd *kissed each other* — just because of the sheer heat and electricity arcing between the two of them. Billy would probably shit kittens if he knew about how they felt and what they'd done.

But what was Kyla feeling about the kiss?

Was it something more?

"Why isn't Kyla seeing anybody, anyway?" Jericho asked. "You said she had a loser boyfriend."

"Yeah. He did a number on her."

Jericho jumped to his feet. "He did *what*?" His hands balled into fists. "Some fucker hurt her?"

"What? No! Relax," Billy said. "What do you think? If somebody tried to hurt her, you think I wouldn't do something? Hell, do you think *she* wouldn't do something? You know how she gets." Billy rolled his eyes. "Seriously. She's sweet until she ain't sweet, and then all hell breaks loose."

Jericho harrumphed. That was true, actually. She was caring until you threatened someone she loved. Then, she got devious. She also had a surprising punch, probably because of all her work in the shop.

"No, the guy was just a loser. A mooch. She did the work, and he was always saying he was working on something. Or he'd be at a job for a few months, then complain about all the ways they were fucked up — because the problem was always them, not him."

Jericho nodded. "I know a few guys like that." They hadn't managed to stay with the crew for long.

"It was a matter of time before the guy started seeing problems in their relationship, and blamed Kyla because she was getting tired of his shit. He moved on to a new girlfriend, and Kyla just focused on the shop. I think that was when she really got into the dress-up crap, too."

Jericho nodded. That would make sense. Kyla wouldn't stay in a slump. She was always moving. She made things happen. He admired that about her.

Billy sighed. "Anyway, you know how she is. She lets people run all over her. She needs to stand up for herself more."

Jericho stared at Billy for a second. "You mean, like you?"

"What? What are you talking about?"

Jericho raised an eyebrow. "You go on vacations."

"Ah, hell..." Billy scowled. "Not you, too."

"You let her run the business end..."

"Because she's better at it!" Billy's eyes narrowed. "Is that why you've stayed for this long? And why you told her that she didn't have to work in the shop? Is she making me look like a dick?"

Jericho sighed. "I'm helping her because she needs the help," he said.

A truck honked outside. Billy grumped. "That's Lindsay," he said. Since he'd broken his right arm, he couldn't drive his stick-shift easily, and Lindsay had prevented him from trying anyway. "Listen, don't feel sorry for Kyla. She can handle herself. She doesn't need you rescuing her."

Jericho frowned as he saw his friend jump in the truck and drive off with his girlfriend. Kyla could handle herself. She was sweet, but she was also very strong, emotionally.

That said, she deserved more than he could give her. He was still a mess emotionally, even if he was figuring it out.

He was going to try talking to his family. To his mother.

He might as well tackle dealing with Kyla, he thought.

He closed the shop, then went upstairs. Kyla was at the kitchen table, sketches strewn around her. Male costumes, notes.

"You okay?" he asked.

She looked up, eyes dazed. Then she focused, and he saw a blush creeping up her cheeks. "Oh. Yeah. Great. You?"

He felt his body tighten. "Um... yeah." He took a deep breath. "We need to talk."

Her expression turned alarmed. "That's never good," she murmured.

"About this morning," he said. "It was..."

Sexual. Sensual. Fucking awesome.

"Unexpected," he said instead, but still heard the strain in his voice.

"True," she agreed.

He looked down at himself. "Listen, let me jump into the shower. Give me five minutes. I don't want... that is, I just..." He swallowed. "I think we should sort of discuss what happened. You know. Like normal adult people."

God, could he screw this up any worse?

She looked down at the table, then looked back at him, her eyes gleaming, her smile broad. He wondered absently if she was doing kegels.

Then his dick started to harden, because the thought of her doing kegels... *oh, man.*

"Five minutes," he repeated.

"Okay," she said brightly.

He took the world's quickest shower. Another cold one. It barely took the edge off.

Why didn't you just say kissing had been a bad idea? he scolded himself as he toweled off. Why didn't he just say that they should stay friends, and keep the physical out of it?

Because you know you want her, his body answered. And it was true. He still wanted her. He knew he shouldn't. He knew she deserved better... someone who would stay, who would put her first.

But damn it, he didn't want her to think he didn't want her.

He realized he'd jumped in the shower without grabbing clean clothes. Cursing his stupidity, he wrapped the towel around his waist, grabbed the bundle of dirty clothes, and headed for the bedroom. "I'll be out in a minute," he called to Kyla, before realizing — she wasn't in the kitchen.

She was in the bedroom. On the bed.

In lingerie.

His mouth went dry, and his eyes widened.

Her white-blonde hair tumbled around her shoulders. Her mouth was a slick, dark pink. Her breasts were barely contained in a silvery-blue bra — one of those half-cup deals that put her on display like his own personal tasting menu — and her matching panties showed off all her moon-pale, smooth, perfect skin.

He dropped the dirty clothes, clutching at his towel.

"Okay," she said, with a smile. "Let's talk."

・♥・♥・♥・♥・♥・

Kyla was shivering with a combination of desire and nerves. Especially when she noticed he was just wearing a towel.

Mercy!

She knew that Jericho was interested, even if he was also conflicted. He probably felt guilty, and confused.

Then she remembered the sheer heat of their kiss that morning, and made up her mind. She wanted him, he wanted her — or at least, he had that morning. But she hadn't tried actively seducing him before.

What if he thought it was a joke, like their usual? What if he'd changed his mind?

If he laughed, she thought with an internal wince, she would die. It didn't even bear thinking about.

He was silent for a long moment, staring at her.

"Seriously, though. We can, erm, discuss. Like normal adult people," she echoed, the words feeling thick and alien coming out of her mouth.

He blinked at her, then she saw his Adam's apple bob as he swallowed hard. "Sorry, what?" he croaked.

She smiled, feeling a shimmer of pleasure at his bewildered, confused state. "Talk," she repeated slowly. "You know. About the sex we're going to be having."

His responding smile was slow and it burned her right down to the tips of her toes. He was freshly showered, and she could see his towel start to tent out in front. *Now, there's a good sign.* "So, you want a safe word or something?" His voice was raspy. He was joking.

Wasn't he?

"Not unless you get one, too," she replied, and her voice sounded ridiculously husky to her own ears, not her usual breathy, somewhat high-pitched tone. She cleared her throat. "But, seriously. I want to have sex with you. I'd like to think you want the same."

"God, yes," he breathed, and she felt tingles all over her body in response.

"Just a quick talk," she said. "You know. So there isn't any, um, weirdness."

"Okay," he said, moving over to the side of the bed, his gaze traveling all over her. It was edging toward summer, and daylight was still bright through the gauzy privacy curtain above the air conditioner. She squirmed, feeling a little self-conscious. She noticed he swallowed again. "What do we need to talk about?"

She sighed. This was the hard part. It'd be easier to just see where it led, but Mallory was right: if she set ground rules, protected herself up front, said it, then she wouldn't have to worry about misunderstandings down the road... or a broken heart. Good fences made good neighbors, she told herself. "Jericho, I've known you and loved you forever."

Now his eyes widened, and he looked slightly panicked. *This is why you don't mention love*, she thought. She stroked his cheek, calming him. "Loved you as a *friend*. You are one of my favorite people, and I don't want things to be weird between us just because we're going to have sex, okay?"

He seemed to relax a little. "You're one of my favorite people, too," he said. "I missed you."

Not enough to visit before now, she thought. *Not enough to stay*. She felt sure her smile was lopsided and bittersweet. "Missed you, too," she said. "I especially love that, even if I haven't seen you for nine years, it snaps right back to being able to hang out with you as if I just saw you yesterday. I value that. And if sex is going to make that weird, then I don't want to do it."

"It won't be weird," he said firmly. Then he kissed her shoulder, stroking his fingertips up and down her forearm, causing the skin to goose-bump. "I was worried about that, too."

"You were?"

"I did think about this, you know," he chastised her gently, walking towards the bed. "But it won't. I promise."

"I know it won't," she said, then let out a little huff. "That's what I'm proposing. You're only going to be here for another two weeks. As long as you're here, we can hook up — as long as we're both interested, obviously."

"I am definitely interested," he said. He was by the side of the bed now, moving towards her, the towel starting to drop a little. She swallowed hard at the visible, sizable bulge she was seeing. "In case you were wondering."

She continued quickly. "It's nobody else's business, and we won't talk about it. When I'm done with the convention and you leave, that's the end of it."

He frowned, sitting beside her. "That's pretty cut and dried. You seem to have given this a lot of thought."

"I'll be honest. If I don't lay down some ground rules, I'll get mixed up," she said. "Sex isn't something I take lightly."

"Hey, I don't, either."

"You're probably not the type for serious relationships, though."

He looked grumpy, distracted. "What makes you say that?"

"I just said I loved you," she said with a chuckle. "And your eyes wheeled like a cow in a slaughterhouse."

He let out a staccato burst of surprised laughter. "I did not."

"You panicked," she said. "You don't want a relationship, do you?"

He looked away, wincing. She took that as a yes, and while she was expecting it, she was still surprised by the sting.

"And I don't want this to get weird because my feelings get confused that we're more than friends or anything. Okay? So just till you leave, and we're done."

He looked at her, still stroking her, his face contemplative. "Would you want more than that?" he asked, his voice low.

She bit her lip. "I don't know," she said. "I know that right now I want you more than I've ever wanted anything or anyone in my life. And if you're half as good as I think you are, I think you're as addictive as blue meth, and that could be... problematic. You know. Long term."

He smiled but still somehow looked sad.

She leaned over and kissed him. "Maybe I should've just gone with it," she said. "But I don't want to get hurt, Jericho. I know you'd never mean to. I still need to take care of myself."

He nodded slowly. "I should leave you alone," he murmured, stroking the side of her face, his face only a breath away from hers. He traced light kisses against her jawline. "You're right. I don't want to hurt you. But I don't know about relationships. And I don't think I could stay, not with all the history I have here in Snoqualmie."

She felt her heart hurt, just a little.

"But I'm not that much of a gentleman," he said, nipping at her earlobe, his hot breath on the bit of flesh where her chin met her neck. "And God, I have never wanted anyone like I want you, either."

He let the towel fall and looked at her for a long moment. She fought the urge to try and pose or fruitlessly suck in her tummy. At size eighteen, she was curvy. She knew that wasn't everybody's cup of tea. If Jericho had a problem with it, though, he probably wouldn't be acting the way he had. Wouldn't have kissed her like that.

Besides, she was a little busy staring at *him* to worry about it.

He was, in a word, gorgeous. The breadth of his chest, the muscularity of his body, covered by the expanse of his deep amber skin. He was probably the stereotypical hot guy, the one you'd put in a calendar holding a puppy or something, the one all women drooled over and wanted.

But he was here, with *her*. Sliding against her, using those long, rough-yet-nimble fingers to skim over her skin. Staring into her eyes. Her traced over her curves, the slope of her hips, the flare of her thighs. He even tickled the back of her knee, surprising her into a giggle.

"Your skin is so soft," he said as his hands traveled back up. "I don't even have words for it. You're like... water. Flower petals. Clouds."

She decided to take the opportunity to do some touching of her own, reaching for him slowly even though sexual hunger was starting to pound through her pulse. She stroked his chest, feeling the coarse sprinkling of hair. He leaned down on one arm, stretching out beside her on the big bed.

Then he kissed her mouth, and all gentleness and slow exploration was burned away in a flash of heat.

She trembled. The feel of him, pressing her down into the pillow with the sheer force of his kiss, was breathtaking. She wove her fingers into his hair, pulling him harder against her, and she felt as well as heard him groan against her mouth. Since her hands were otherwise occupied, she continued stroking him, only now with her entire body. Her thighs spread, her leg caressing his, her foot twining behind his calf. She could feel the hot, hard head of his cock brushing against her thigh.

He tore his mouth away with a growl and moved down, lower, tugging her demi-cup down in a quick, rough motion. He took one of her breasts into his mouth and sucked hard enough for her to feel currents of lust shooting from her nipples to between her legs, which were already slick. She could feel her panties drenched in it, her thighs coating with it. She moved restlessly against him.

"Jericho," she murmured, arching her back. Releasing his hair, she kneaded his shoulders and wriggled, slowly but surely maneuvering him between her thighs. Then she reached behind her, clumsily unhooking her bra. He released her long enough to remove it, tossing it blindly to one side.

He switched breasts, one hand positioning it to his mouth, the other propping him up so he was half on, half off of her body. "Holy shit," he breathed frantically against the side of her breast, nipping at her so that she jumped. "Kyla. God, you feel amazing."

"So do you," she gasped. She felt the head of his cock brush against her wetness, and she shivered, trying to angle him in. She shifted slightly, hugging his length, causing him to groan. He nudged against her, his hips flexing, his cock pressing against the thin silk barrier between them.

"Jericho," she whimpered now. Her body pulsed for him. She felt empty. She wanted to feel his hot, hard length inside her.

"Slow down, sweetheart," he growled. "You are nowhere near ready for me yet."

"Spoken like a man," she said, and did a roll of her hips, smiling at his resulting moan. "I want you now. I want to feel you. I can take it."

"Don't worry," he murmured, sounding confident. "You'll like this."

He pulled away, and she wanted to scream. He kissed down her stomach, his fingertips biting into her hips. He slipped off her panties until she was naked beneath him. His mouth went lower...

"Oh!" She jolted. His fingertips parted the curls that covered her, and his tongue traced the tip of her wet slit. She felt unaccountably nervous. She'd never been one for oral sex. Her boyfriend in high school had considered himself a master, but honestly, she hadn't gotten much out of it and had usually faked an orgasm just to get it over with. Subsequent boyfriends might've given a token offer for oral, but they were unenthusiastic, which made her self-conscious, or unskilled, which left her unsatisfied and frustrated. But Jericho...

He looked like he was kissing her reverently, his eyes closed, his mouth working gently. His tongue delved between her now swollen folds, almost tickling before licking deeper, until he found her clit. He worked slowly, steadily, lavishing attention, until she felt like it was a hard button of pleasure. She was panting in time with his gentle exploration.

Then he took that erect nub of pleasure into his mouth, slid his tongue in deeper, and *sucked*.

She felt her eyes roll back in her head, and she let out a squeak of shock.

His laugh reverberated against her flesh. The suction increased, and his tongue — holy cannoli, that tongue — plunged into her. His teeth scraped her clit slightly, and then he returned, circling, sucking, penetrating.

She felt her body start to tighten, and she rolled her head from one side to the other as pressure built.

She felt herself start to clench... and he pushed one finger inside.

She came with a scream, and she heard him groan, felt his hips pressing against the bed in time with his finger. She all but sobbed his name.

He wiped his mouth with his arm, smirking. "I take it you like oral," he said smugly.

She heaved a deep breath. "Well, I do *now*."

"Any time you want me to go down on you, I'll be happy to." He kissed her thighs, her hips, stroking her legs. "You taste fantastic."

"Turnabout's fair play," she said, wanting to catch up... wanting to help him feel as good as he'd made her feel.

"Maybe later," he said, reaching over to the nightstand. "Holy shit, I almost came on the bed. Never enjoyed it as much as that before. I want to be inside you."

Just like that, her body rebounded, clamoring at the idea. "Yes," she agreed, stroking his hip, the tight muscles of his back. "Oh, yes."

He froze. "Uh, I don't have any protection. I don't suppose...?"

She smiled, quickly reaching over to a nightstand. "Condom," she said, tossing him one. "Like I said — safety first."

"Absolutely." He rolled on the condom, and she was amazed to find his hands were shaking. He was just as turned on as she was, she thought. Which turned her on even more.

"I'll try to make it last, but Jesus, I think this is gonna be quick," he grunted as he rolled on top of her. His skin felt blazing-hot and all-encompassing. "Jesus, Ky, I want you."

"Please," she breathed, opening herself up to him. She could feel the strength and flex of his arm as he reached between them, positioning his cock where she needed it the most. She parted her thighs, cradling him, and she felt the broad, blunt head of him at her entrance.

Then he moved in, gliding from the wetness of her previous orgasm.

There was a *lot* of him, she couldn't help but notice. She felt the pressure, wall to wall, and gasped.

"You all right?" he said, holding still.

"Yeah," she choked. "I'm... You're just.. It's been awhile."

"All right," he said, and he sounded strained. "Can you take the rest?"

"You mean there's *more*?"

His laugh sounded pained. "Yup. Like I said, you needed to be ready."

"Oh...kay."

He slowly inched in, and she felt remarkably filled. She shifted experimentally and felt him brush against a spot that had her gasping and panting as her nerve endings caught fire in the best possible way. "Oh, God," she murmured, shifting and squirming against that delicious ache. "Oh, my *God*."

"Kyla?" he said, pulling back a little, sounding concerned.

"Oh my God, you feel... so... *good*," she said, wrapping her legs around him and pulling at his shoulders. "Please. Please!"

He pressed forward, and she felt it again. She was breathing hard, like she'd just run a marathon, muttering wild, incoherent noises of desire and pleasure. Sounds that got progressively more hoarse and filthy as he continued to withdraw and press, retreat and surge forward.

Within minutes, his breathing was as racked and frantic as hers. He wasn't being careful, and she didn't care. He was groaning, slamming into her sheath, and she was meeting every thrust as shock and thrill shot through her.

The orgasm was enormous. She might have screamed. She definitely yelled Jericho's name as pulse after pulse rammed through her, wringing her out like a towel. She barely registered his shout of climax as his hips pounded against her, triggering a strong aftershock of pleasure of her own.

In the aftermath, she was breathing hard, feeling reborn. Crazy.

She'd probably made the worst mistake of her life. But she couldn't help herself. And she was definitely going to enjoy the rest of their time together.

No matter how much it hurt once he was gone.

CHAPTER 8

Kyla woke up slowly, with a surreal sense of disbelief. Jericho's naked body was pressed against her, his muscular arm around her waist, his breath whooshing softly in and out behind her ear. She wiggled experimentally. His long, hard cock was also pressing against her thighs.

Her whole body tingled. She was very, very tempted to take advantage of his hardness, she realized. Even if they'd had sex twice already the night before.

Who wants to go for a hat trick? It's not like three would *kill* her, right?

He must've felt her waking, because he started kissing her shoulder and her neck. "Morning," he rumbled, and she shivered.

Sexy. The man was so intensely, insanely sexy.

"What are your plans for today?" he said, this time adding some nibbles behind her ear.

"Honestly, I was thinking of just turning over, grabbing the entire box of condoms, and hanging the "closed" sign in the shop and simply having sex with you until I pass out. That okay with you?

But that wasn't the point here. She had a limited amount of time before he left. And he was going to leave. She had one shot to make this costume business work. Sure, she could keep plugging away in off hours, but somehow, she'd made this into a big final push. If she could win the contest, if she could just get the attention, she could make enough money to show Billy that this wasn't just playing dress. She could justify to her family that she wasn't ungrateful for them passing the business on. It was her key, her way out.

Sighing, she moved towards the side of the bed, away from the temptation of his body.

"Where do you think you're going?" he growled tugging her back to him. Oh, for the love of God, that hard-on. She felt her resolve starting to melt away. "I wasn't through with you yet."

Her body fought mutinously, but she tightened her resolve. "I'm not through with you yet, either," she said, her voice deep and raspy as Jessica Rabbit's. "But it's Thursday. I've got a ton of work today if I'm going to meet that deadline. And you've still got the shop to run, right?"

He stroked at her stomach, kissing his way down her spine. "It can wait."

His mouth... she bit her lip. "I have three male costumes to somehow figure out how to make in the next two weeks," she said, her eyes fluttering as he stroked between her sensitive thighs with the fat head of his cock. "I could throw something together, but I want to win this thing, and some thrown together costumes aren't going to get that done. I need them to be up to my standards, and I need to find models for them, too. So... oh God, don't do that," she said, trembling as he nudged her opening.

"Three male models, huh?" he said, fitting his body to hers from the back, rubbing and massaging her breasts and gently tugging on the nipples. She felt her eyes roll back in her head. "What kind of costumes were you thinking?"

"I can't think at all when you do that," she gasped, pushing her ass back to meet him. "I... Oh, God. Um. I don't know."

"Have you made any costumes for guys before?"

How was he forming sentences when she could barely remember her name? She struggled for coherence. "Uh... I have made some male costumes before. Mostly for Mallory, though."

Jericho paused for a second, his hands cupping her breasts. "Mallory's a guy?"

"Genderfluid-ish," she said, writhing. "I made her a Malcolm Reynolds cosplay from *Firefly* that's pretty awesome."

"Maybe you can ask the contest coordinator if it has to be a guy in costume, or if the costume just needs to be considered, you know, male."

"As long as they don't consider it genderbend, it might pass. That's good," she said, again starting to pull away again, only to have him press forward. She backed up, her thighs clenching against his naked cock. "Really, really good..."

"Know anybody else who might act as a model?"

"I... God, I don't know." She felt her resistance starting to melt away. "I need you."

"I'm just trying to help, babe." She could hear rather than see the smugness of his expression, since her eyes were closed. She was lost in the sensations his hands and mouth and body were causing.

"I... uh. Hailey might know some people," she babbled. "And Tessa. She works in a company full of guys. I'm pretty sure I could recruit a guy or two from there. She's been trying to set me up on dates with a few of them."

She felt him freeze. "Oh?"

She took the opportunity to scoot a little further from him, getting some of her thoughts under control. "Jose Yao is really into fantasy, now that I think about it. Maybe Abraham — he's kind of an ass, total Alpha male, but he's really tall and ripped."

"Ripped." Jericho's eyes went hooded. "Really."

"Yeah. Now that I think of it, I should probably pick somebody who could play Khal Drogo. I need to make a couple costume, and I'm going as Daenerys Stormborn." She frowned, biting her lip as her brain kicked into overdrive. That was definitely a possible solution, one she should've thought of herself. Jose was probably a great candidate — he loved cosplay, hit a lot of the conventions. She still hadn't quite forgiven Abraham for being such an ass to Tessa last year, though, even if he was a better physical fit for Drogo than Jose was.

She was abruptly jarred back when Jericho all but tackled her, caging her with his body. "Tryin' to make me jealous?"

"What?" she yelped, stunned.

"These guys that you could be dating, guys that are 'really ripped' and into fantasies," he growled. "Saying you're going to play part of a couple with one of these men."

"So? It's just pretend!"

"You just had sex with me." His eyes almost glowed, and you could make s'mores off the heat that was coming off his body. "And will again."

She frowned. "What, exactly, is the problem here?"

"The problem is, I want to bury myself in you," he said, "and it's making me crazy to hear about you talking about other guys. Even though it's not my place."

She felt a shiver at his words. She knew she shouldn't read into them — she wouldn't like it, either, if he talked about other women when she was really turned on. And she wasn't the type of person who found jealousy a turn-on. But that little bit of possessiveness had her engine revving even a little more than it already was.

Bracing herself, she rolled, nudging him onto his back. "Let's get a couple of things straight, okay? Remember the ground rules? This goes on as long as you're here." She straddled him, his cock tucked just in front of her, rubbing against her clit. Don't think about it, she scolded herself. Not until this was done. "Second of all: as long as

I'm with you, I'm not going to be with anyone else, in any way. Okay?"

He nodded. "I know, I feel like an idiot..."

"Finally, I'm not looking for a relationship right now." Okay, that was a bit of a lie. She wanted a relationship, but it was with somebody completely unattainable, so she wasn't going to think about it. "I want to make the costume business work. So, all I'm thinking about is how to meet the deadline, and that can make me kind of focused. When I get closer to deadline, I will get progressively crazy, which I apologize for in advance. So if you want to help, either find me a model, or be one."

"Be a model?" His voice pitched a little higher with obvious surprise. "Me?"

"Yup."

"I'll think about it," he muttered. "All right, problems mostly solved. How about some sex, then? Just to tide us over until tonight?" His voice sounded hopeful.

"I should make you wait," she said. Then shook her head. "But that'll distract me, too."

"Just gonna use me, huh?" He said it with a grin, though, so she knew he wasn't insulted.

"Shush." She pulled out a condom and a box of cinnamon mints, grabbing some. He grabbed a few as well, crunching them. Morning breath conquered, she sheathed him and then, without ado, impaled herself on him.

"Oh, God," she said. "How are you this good?" It wasn't his size, or not just his size. It was everything about him.

"You fit me so well. So fucking well," he groaned, sitting up against the headboard and tugging her closer to him. She wrapped her legs around his waist, and he lifted his hips, the rolling motion plunging inside her, rubbing his pubic bone against her clit. Soon, they were gasping against each other. She swiveled her hips, and he bit her neck. She knew he'd leave marks. She didn't even care.

It was building up, she knew it. She could feel her body clenching tightly, felt him starting to lose control, his measured movements going more frenzied and clumsy. She scratched down his back, bucking against him.

"So good," she gasped. "So good..."

"Kyla," he yelled, slamming into her, and she shouted as her orgasm pounded through her, her eyes clenching shut and going black as her whole body convulsed. She could feel his heaviness all against her, and she kept rocking against him as he shuddered inside her, holding her tight, their bodies slick with sweat.

She rested her head against his shoulder. It had never been like this with anyone before. She worried that it might never be like this with anyone again.

You have two weeks, she thought. *Two weeks to follow your dream. Two weeks with him.*

Make it count.

Slowly, she disentangled herself from him, kissing him softly.

"All right," she said. "I've got work to do."

· ♥ · ♥ · ♥ · ♥ · ♥ ·

That Monday morning, after he'd finally managed to get himself out of Kyla's apartment without sexually devouring her – *again* – he had an even more difficult time getting her out of his head. He'd always enjoyed sex, and it had been a while for him, but that didn't explain the compulsion he had to be with her. Maybe it was the contradiction of her, innocent and sweet and sunshiny but with a dirty streak and an earthy sensuality that made him want to beg for more. Maybe because he'd known her for a long time, and more to the point, she knew him: all his weaknesses, all his faults and frailties. And she still cared about him. He wasn't sure what it was, but he wanted to investigate, that was for damned certain.

And you've got about two weeks to do it.

"Hey dude. You okay?"

He jolted, smacking his head on the raised bumper of the Chrysler on the lift. "Jesus."

Billy laughed. "Jumpy much?"

Jericho rubbed at his head. "What? No. Never mind."

Billy's eyes narrowed and the laugh died. "What's wrong?"

"Nothing's wrong."

"Yeah it is." Billy frowned. "You're acting weird, and you look like you did when we borrowed my Dad's 50cc to off-road out by the river."

"*Borrowed*," Jericho corrected. "We brought it back."

Billy ignored him. "What did you do now?"

Jericho winced. "I... um..."

I may have had sex with your sister.

"I'm going to go see my Mom today."

Jericho blinked. He was just as surprised at the words coming out of his mouth as Billy seemed to be.

"Really? Why?"

Jericho frowned. Why the hell was he? "It's like we talked about last night. I gotta get over this shit."

"Okay." Billy still didn't look convinced. "Well... good luck with that, I guess. You going tonight or something?"

"I'm going to take a long lunch and ride over," Jericho said, thinking the plan through. He didn't want to deal with his mother and Gary at the same time. Gary was a nice guy, and maybe that was part of the problem – he'd always been so damned nice, helpful. Almost alien to the teen Jericho had been. He'd certainly been at a loss when dealing with the pitched fights between Jericho and his mother. Better to just deal with her head on, he reasoned.

His stomach knotted. Hopefully, it wouldn't be a repeat of those painful sessions.

Besides, he wanted to save nights for Kyla. He knew she'd have to work, but he also knew that whatever time she could spare, whenever she was ready, he wanted to fill. When she wasn't working on her costumes, they would be together.

At noon, Jericho rode up to the nondescript house in Carnation, just a little down the river from Snoqualmie. It was one story. There was a tire swing on a large maple tree in the backyard. He parked the motorcycle and felt his nerves jittering as he walked up to the front door.

His mother answered it. "I just got Sammy down to sleep," she said, ushering him in.

He grimaced. "My bike didn't wake him up, did it?"

"Oh, don't worry. Once he's asleep, he sleeps like a rock," she assured him. "It's getting him to sleep that's the trick."

Jericho fidgeted. He wondered if he should've brought something, like... he didn't know. Flowers? A card?

Kyla would've known. He should've asked her. Hell, he should've *brought* her, he thought, then shook the thought off. She didn't have time. She needed to work on the costumes. Besides that, she wasn't his girlfriend, and that was probably the sort of thing a girlfriend would do.

He wasn't going to take advantage of her that way.

His mother's face was drawn, and he sensed her nervousness, as well. "Can I get you a cup of coffee or something?" she said.

"I'd... Sure. That sounds good," he said. "But I can't take too long. I need to get back to the Summers' auto shop."

"You always did like spending time with them," she said. He braced himself for sourness, for accusation, but her statement seemed harmless. She went and made the coffee in the kitchen, and he followed her in, shifting his weight nervously. "How are they? The Summers, I mean?"

"Doing well. Their parents retired, so it's Kyla and Billy running the shop now. Billy broke his arm skiing, so Kyla called me and asked if I could come out and help."

They fell into silence, the only sound the coffee dripping through the machine into the glass pot. It was torturous.

"How is it having a kid again?" he finally blurted out.

She leaned against the counter. "Good. Different." She sighed. "I was only sixteen when I had you, Jericho. I was thirty-nine when I had Sammy. It was a very different experience." She smiled ruefully. "You were both surprises, though."

Jericho squirmed. "Too much info, Mom."

She laughed, and he found himself grinning back at her.

"How are you doing?" he asked. "Still working?"

She shook her head. "I'm lucky. Gary's job is doing great, and we were able to buy this house before prices went up. I'm a stay-at-home Mom now." She let out a breath. "I worked so hard when you were a kid, and left you with your grandparents so much. I want to spend this time with him. Not..."

Jericho gritted his teeth. "Not make the same mistakes, huh?"

She reddened. "You were never a mistake," she said quietly. "A surprise isn't a mistake."

He shrugged. "It's good, though. That's good." He struggled to shift the topic to something less painful. "How is grandma?"

"Older. Not as able to keep up with her grandson as she was when you were Sammy's age." She smiled. "It's harder for me, too. Can't really pull all-nighters and go without sleep."

"Yeah. I'm not as into partying as much as I was as a kid, either."

He noticed the concern in her eyes, the curiosity, but she just looked down at her empty coffee cup. "How are you?" she asked, her voice serious. "I don't want to pry, or drive you away. I just... I want to make sure you're all right."

"I'm all right," he said, then took a deep breath. "I'm sorry, Mom. Sorry that I never called. You had to be fuc..." He quickly cleared his throat, cutting off the cuss that threatened. "You had to be *really* worried about me. Hell, I was at an age where I could've made stupid decisions."

His mother's brown eyes clouded with tears. "I was worried," she said. "You'll never have any idea. At least, I pray you never do."

His shoulders hunched. "I got lucky, and fell in with a really good group. But I still should've contacted you. I was pissed, and self-righteous, and I was stupid. And I'm sorry."

He was surprised at how easily the apology came out of his mouth. He was downright shocked at the feeling of lightness that resulted. He was almost dizzy with the relief of his apology.

The tears spilled over on her cheeks. "I am so sorry, Jericho," his mother said. "I didn't know what to do, and I kept seeing you move further and further away from me and I just felt so out of control. I was working hard, even after I married Gary, to make sure our life was better. And you weren't responding to him, and you were treating me like a stranger in our own home." She took a deep breath. "I was scared, and that is my fault. I didn't like what you were doing, and I felt disrespected and confused. But that's not good enough, I know. I let us drift apart. I kept thinking you'd come around to seeing my way to do things. I thought if I was just harsher with you, you'd 'straighten up.' But it never worked that way."

He nodded.

"Therapy showed me that I was doing what your grandfather had done most of his life," she said, and he looked at her with surprise. He hadn't really thought about it, but his grandfather had been a stern guy. He'd died when Jericho was maybe six or so, so his memories of the man weren't that clear.

"Kicking you out was the worst, most stupid thing I have ever done," his mother finally said. "I have regretted the words I said that day every day since you left."

He bowed his head. "In your defense, I was a little shit," he said, surprising a little burble of laughter out of her.

"No. I mean, yes, you were kind of," she admitted, and he chuckled. "You didn't want to listen. You were headstrong. You had your own ideas of what you wanted to do and what you wanted to be." She took a deep breath. "You're just like I was at your age."

"Really?" It occurred to him – he'd never really asked his mother what her life was like at his age. He only knew of her as the woman who prevented him from having fun, the task master, the pain in the ass. Not as the human.

She poured coffee, putting it on the table in front of him. He turned down cream and sugar. She sat across from him with her own mug. She'd aged, he noticed — of course she would have. She had a few more lines, several gray hairs lacing through the black. Smile lines, though, as well as worry lines. He didn't resent the lines. If anything, he was glad she'd had happiness.

"I didn't want to listen to my parents. I went looking for trouble," she said. "I was hanging out with wild kids. It wasn't even like I was hanging out at the rez, because we weren't on the rez. Snoqualmie didn't have one, and my father — your grandfather — didn't want to go to the Tulalip one."

"He was bitter about that," Jericho said, suddenly remembering. "I never really understood why."

"The tribe's history is... complicated," she said, and the sorrow deepened. "I'd like to think that they're settling down, that things are improving. I'd also like to think that I'm contributing to that. When your grandfather died, your grandmother and I both swore that we'd get you involved in the tribe and help you get to know your people. But I think it might've been too late. You were already too into motorcycles, and doing your own thing."

"I..." He swallowed a scalding sip of coffee, unsure of what to say. "I'm sorry," he finally said. It felt like too little.

"It's not your fault," she said.

"I never knew my father," he said slowly. "But... I don't know. It always felt like I wasn't white enough for the white kids. And the tribal kids knew I was white. It was like I couldn't win."

She sniffed. "I know. And I am so, so sorry. Not that you were born — although that was my own fault. But that I was too young to know how to deal with you, how to take care of you better."

He shook his head. "I am sorry I was a pain in the ass."

She smiled, a watery smile. "I'm glad you came back," she said. "I'm glad I can talk to you. I've missed you, Jericho."

He felt his heart crack, just a little. "Missed you too," he muttered.

She shifted. "I... I don't want to drive you away," she said. "I won't ask you about what you're doing."

He sat up. She thought he was a one percenter, he realized. And she wasn't going to say a damned thing about it. She was trying so fucking hard not to judge him.

Just like that, more of his past resentments dissolved.

"I'm not in a gang or anything, Mom," he said quickly, and the relief that shot through her expression made his chest ache. "I mean, I don't have a nine-to-five job or anything, but I'm not into drugs or gun running or any of the shi... of the crap you see on TV," he said.

She slumped a little in her chair. "Oh?" she said weakly, obviously trying to be casual.

"Going off, wanting to quit school... It wasn't to be a biker. I mean, yeah, part of it was probably like that. I wanted to be a badass. I found these guys that I felt like I fit in with," he admitted. "But it was more because I loved bikes. I loved engines. Working on things. And I found a group that felt like I did. That's what I felt with the Summers, as well."

She nodded slowly. "Your father loved his motorcycle," she said. "He could fix anything, his friends said. But he was in a gang, and he would do anything for them. They certainly meant more to him than I did." She shrugged. "He left before I could tell him I was pregnant. I never knew how to find him again. I heard that he'd died, but I never knew for sure."

Jericho stiffened. "You never told me that."

"I should have," she said. "But the more you got involved with engines and motorcycles, the more I could see the future for you — and the more scared I was for you."

Suddenly, things made sense. All the fights they'd had. The dire predictions she had made for him: "*You'll be a thug! You won't amount to anything!*"

She wasn't yelling at him, or at least, not just at him. She'd been yelling at a ghost.

"I work on custom bikes," he said. "I travel around a lot. I've seen a lot of the country. But I'm careful, and I'm not a thug."

She hung her head. "I never should have called you that."

"You didn't know," he said, and he felt forgiveness envelope him like a blanket... envelope them both. "I love you, Mom. I didn't get it before, but I see now what you were trying to do. And I'm really, really sorry I was a stupid kid."

She got up, crying, and hugged him. He stroked her hair. He dwarfed her now, he realized. She seemed so tiny.

"You're not going to disappear again, are you?" she asked.

He felt guilt pierce him again. "I'm not staying," he said, and she held him a little tighter, just for a second, before letting him go. "But I promise: I'll make sure you can always reach me."

She looked a little nervous, and he stared at her until she nodded.

"I *promise*, Mom."

She smiled, brushing at the tears on her eyelashes. "I love you, too. And I'm glad you came back."

He hugged her, and realized – he was glad, too.

· ♥ · ♥ · ♥ · ♥ · ♥ ·

"I really appreciate you helping me out with this, Abraham," Kyla said, feeling uncomfortable. "I was working on a larger scale for a client when I started this outfit, and I'd forgotten about it. I think you'll fit it best."

Abraham shrugged. He wasn't as physically imposing as Jericho (then again, few men were), but he was about six feet tall and bulky in a muscular way, not fat. She got the feeling he lifted weights or did Crossfit or something. "I owe Tessa," he said. "Lost another bet."

She laughed, she couldn't help it, but quickly buttoned it when he scowled. "Sorry to hear that."

"I underestimated how good she was at *Overwatch*," he admitted, then shrugged.

She pondered logistics of how to do this, then decided to just jump right in. "Go ahead into the sewing room. I need you to stand there, so I can measure you."

"Okay." Obediently, he stepped into the center of the chaotic mess.

She sighed. *And now, the awkwardness.* "Um... in your boxers. Just your boxers."

His eyes opened wider, then he grinned, a surprisingly attractive grin, his teeth flashing from inside his auburn goatee. "Oh-kay," he drawled.

"I need to measure you," she explained.

"Measure me, huh?" He grabbed the back of his T-shirt and pulled it over his head. Guy had a nice chest, she had to admit. Not for her, but he'd make some girl happy. "Sure you got a big enough tape there, sweetie?"

She rolled her eyes. "Don't get ideas, cowboy, or I will stick you with pins. Got it?"

"Hey, whatever floats your boat." He stripped out of his shoes and pants, leaving him in plaid boxers and a grin.

A year before, she'd started working on an *Assassin's Creed* outfit for a guy, making up the vambraces and some of the detail work to show how it could be done. It was good practice. The guy was on the bigger side – more "Dad bod" than "hot bod" – and he'd balked when she told him the price for that level of authenticity. He wanted kick ass cosplay for nearly nothing, and she'd decided to keep it, but had never continued working on it. Now, she prayed it was far enough along to finish in the time allotted.

She looked at Abraham critically, comparing his build to the pattern pieces. "I'll need to make the jacket bigger," she muttered to herself, draping the tape measure around her neck and studying his build. "Accommodate the shoulders, make sure those double cap sleeves fit. Already have the buttons, the vambraces. Bring in the waist a little, although — fuck it, I can just handle that with the wide belt, it'll save time. The leather pauldron cape should work fine as is. And I need to take the tasers out of the hidden blades, but other than that, I can just do detailing..."

"Back up," Abraham interrupted. "Did you just say *tasers?*"

Thrown off her game, she looked up. "Huh? Oh, yeah. I made those for Hailey, one of the Frost sisters. She got attacked by that stalker last year..."

"Yeah, I heard about that," Abraham said, frowning. "That was fucked up. She got cut, right?"

"Yes." Kyla's blood still ran cold remembering the incident. "Anyway, after that, I decided to make her some things. We wound up getting her pepper spray and the tasers didn't really work out as planned because she doesn't wear loose enough clothing. I can still use the mechanics for this costume, though." She realized she was rambling. "Anyhoo, try on these pants."

She had him pull up the leather pants she'd originally sewn together, but she knew immediately it wasn't going to work. "I am not going to be able to make alterations to leather. Your thighs are too big, and your waist is too small. The fit is going to be shit," she complained, kneeling down and shaking her head. "Hmmm. I think I'm going to have to just sew some new ones... maybe a brushed denim or something? No. Pleather, something thin, easy to sew. Shit, shit. Need to figure out something easier."

"Kyla? What is going on here?"

She looked up to see Jericho standing in the doorway, looking angry.

"Oh, hey. What time is it? Did you already close the garage?" Her eyes felt sandy with exhaustion, but she knew she had to keep pressing on. "All right. I'm gonna take those measurements, Abraham, okay?"

"You do whatever you want, babe," Abraham almost purred.

"Just step out of the leather," she said, rubbing at her eyes with the heels of her palms.

"Kyla," Jericho ground out.

She looked over her shoulder at him. "What?"

He glared at her. "You've got a dude wearing underwear in your sewing room, and you're kneeling in front of his dick," Jericho said, his voice low.

She stared at him. "That is true, yes."

She heard Abraham chuckling.

Jericho let out a breath. "Can you see why I might be a trifle... concerned here?"

"No, honestly, I can't," she said, with some tartness of her own. "Abraham, can you give us a second here?"

"No problem," he said, smiling like a cat who'd eaten a cream-filled canary. "I'll just be standing here. Without pants."

She rolled her eyes. "Not helping," she muttered, then followed Jericho to the living room. "You know I have to make these costumes. I got Rachel and Hailey down to underwear too, when I made their costumes, if that's any comfort. It's the most accurate way to take measurements, and I don't have the time to mess around with clothes that don't fit, okay?"

Jericho's eyes blazed. "It's different with the girls," he said. "It's just... how would you feel if I were in the same room as a chick in her underwear, my face all by her crotch?"

"One, if I knew it was for something important, I would say exactly nothing," she said. "Two, you're leaving in two weeks. And you can't tell me you haven't been in the same room as chicks in their underwear, or bikinis, or probably even less. True?"

She watched as he winced. "Not since I got here. And sure as hell not now."

That didn't say anything about what would happen when he left.

She couldn't afford to think about it. It would throw her off her game. Instead, she focused, gritting her teeth. "This is important to me. You said you believe in me, and you support me in this. So please, don't be a butthead, okay? I have no time, I am in the zone, and I frankly can't afford the distraction right now."

He blinked, probably in surprise at the sharpness of her tone. Then he reluctantly nodded.

"If you can't handle it, stay out here, or go outside, all right?" Without looking to see if he agreed, she huffed out an impatient breath and headed back to Abraham who was still smirking. "You knock that crap off, too," she warned.

"You are a firecracker," Abraham said. "I like 'em with spirit."

"Spread your legs."

"Like the way this is going." He did as instructed.

She whipped out her tape measure. "Keep being a jerk, and I will show you how sharp my sewing shears are," she threatened. She took his inseam, his waist, his thighs. "Now get your pants back on," she snapped, writing down the measurements. "I'm gonna need you back next week for final fitting, and I'm going to need you to do your little dance on the catwalk for the contest, okay? You're going to convince me you're Ezio frickin' Auditore, from *Assassin's Creed 2*."

"Sure thing, babe."

"And if I lose this because you decided to be cutesy, I am going to cut you."

He laughed. "I really like you."

Her head shot up, and she was ready to snarl at him until he put a surprisingly gentle hand on her wrist.

"Seriously," he said, his voice dropping low. "I like you. That guy seems kinda jealous. Rough, like he likes to get pushy. You need help with him, you want my backup, you let me know."

She blinked. "Help with him? Doing what?" Was he suggesting a threesome or something?

Oh, God, she could *not* deal with this right now.

"If he's threatening you," Abraham clarified, low enough that it wouldn't carry to the kitchen where Jericho was pacing. "Or treating you bad. I promise, I will fuck him up and make him sorry."

She was surprised. No, she was shocked. "Jericho would never hurt me," she said, stunned at the thought.

"If you say so." Abraham didn't sound convinced. "Just say the word if you need help, though."

After a few minutes, she did the measurements, writing down notes. "Got everything. Thanks, Abraham," she said.

"My pleasure," he said, winking and pulling his clothes on with complete aplomb. She saw Jericho glaring from the other room. "Just remember what I told you, girlie," Abraham said, before nodding at Jericho and leaving, closing the door behind him.

She turned to Jericho. "What in the hell..."

He swept her up and she squealed as he carried her to the bedroom.

"What are you doing?" she yelped.

His mouth covered hers in a fierce, passionate kiss. She felt her senses swim and her heart pound. His hands were everywhere at once. The anger at his high-handedness slowly melted away, until she was clawing at him the way he was at her.

His breathing was harsh. "I feel like a caveman. I'm an idiot," he said. "I'm being backward and regressive and you don't deserve it at all, you did absolutely *nothing* wrong. But I swear, if I'm not inside you in the next five seconds, I am gonna punch a hole in a wall. I need to know you're mine, right now."

"Super domination does not do it for me," she said, as he tossed her on the bed, tearing off her T-shirt and unhooking her bra. Then he kissed her again, grinding his hard-on against her until she melted. "Well, not normally anyway," she amended breathlessly. "So don't get used to it."

He stripped off her yoga pants, his mouth going straight to her cleft. He sucked her through her panties and she arched her back, pressing her hips higher against his hungry mouth. "Oh, God."

He was clumsily tearing at his own clothes as he continued to devour her, his tongue pressing against the fabric and piercing her pussy, laving her clit. "You taste so fucking good," he said. She heard the tear of his T-shirt, his swearing. When he left to take off his pants, she leaned up on her elbows to watch. She'd never seen him so ham-handed. He tore at his button-fly, cursing it when it didn't undo as quickly or smoothly as he wanted. He looked like a man possessed.

She would laugh at the picture he made if she wasn't feeling the same way. She'd never, ever had a man want her the way Jericho seemed to. He made her feel desired. He made her feel like she was the only thing he could possibly want, like he'd die if he didn't have her. It went to her head like whiskey, leaving her drunk and reeling and helplessly intoxicated by sensations she couldn't control.

"He can't want you like I want you," he said, fingering her pussy as he sucked first one breast, then the other. She shuddered, her legs jittering as he continued his relentless assault. "I swear, nobody on earth could want you like I want you. You're *mine*."

Even as her body wanted to scream its agreement, her heart pinched.

If you want me that badly, why won't you stay?

She wasn't going to say it. She'd made this agreement. This was sex, and only sex. She had to protect her heart.

She scooted away, ignoring his growl of possession, and twisted onto her stomach, looking at him demurely. "I'm yours," she said, with a taunting pause. "For now."

His eyes lit. He took her in. She smiled at him coquettishly, even as she felt a little frisson of doubt — and a tremor of nerves.

"*Mine*," he repeated. He was staring at her body now. "That ass," he said. "I swear, it will haunt me. It's perfect." He pulled her to him, kneading it, then leaned forward and gnawed at her, dragging his teeth over her skin. She was on all fours, propped up on her elbows and knees. She started to scrabble away, but he wrapped an arm around her waist. "Not so fast," he said.

She widened her legs, stroking the outside of his calves with her own. "Maybe I like it fast."

Before she could say anything, he plunged inside her.

She gasped, then let out a purr of pure pleasure. The feel of him... good god. The smooth glide of...

"Wait," he muttered. "Damn it. Condom, baby."

She tried not to, but her pussy clenched around him, causing them both to groan.

"Are you clean, Jericho?" she heard herself ask, surprising herself.

"Oh, Christ," he breathed. "Yeah. I don't sleep around, always wear protection, and I get tested on the reg. Got results on my phone, if you want."

"I have an IUD," she said. Then waited, reveling in the feel of him, smooth and hard and filling her so completely.

They were silent for a second.

"Are you sure?" he finally asked, his voice strained to the breaking point.

To answer, she pressed back against him, hard.

It was like a dam breaking. He pressed hard against her, and she backed into him, bucking him. He reached around in front her, his long fingers stroking her clit as his mouth pressed hard kisses against her. Most guys didn't get just how much of an erogenous zone a woman's back could be, but he got it. Man, did he get it.

"You feel so damned good," he said, rocking against her, his cock sliding in and out as his fingers worked harder, building the fire inside her more and more. "Like this pussy was made for me. I have never felt like this, not ever. Just want to fuck... you... so hard..."

Their rhythm was harder, pounding. Her breasts swayed beneath her, her muscles straining against him. She screamed as the orgasm took her. "Jericho!"

He groaned, loud and long, but kept grinding against her. He gripped her breasts, pulling her up so she was against his chest, his cock straining against her. She stroked her breasts, tugging at her own nipples. He saw, she knew. He was glancing at her over her shoulder, watching her.

He pulled her down on his massive cock, chanting her name over and over. The second orgasm surprised her, and she clenched. Hard.

He shouted, and she could feel the heat of him coming inside her. She wanted to weep, it felt so good. They both collapsed on her bed. He rolled her to the side, so he wouldn't crush her.

"You are so good, baby," he said, out of breath, still buried inside her. "So fucking good."

She didn't say anything, just rocked against him. "I have more to do tonight," she finally said, after a moment.

He sighed. "I'm sorry I was an asshole earlier," he said. "I don't know where that came from."

She nodded. "Well, I guess you'll have to find some way to make it up to me."

He kissed her, but it wasn't a possessive or punishing kiss. It was sweet, and sexy... and promising.

"With kegels like yours?" he said. "It'll be my pleasure."

CHAPTER 9

It had been just over two weeks since he'd come back to Snoqualmie, and a week since he and Kyla had started sleeping together, and he couldn't believe how much things had changed. Now, he woke up with his arms around Kyla, breathing in her scent and enjoying the feel of her soft skin beneath his fingers. Then, after some nuzzling (and some shower sex, as quietly as possible in case Billy was already in the shop), he went down to the shop and worked on cars while Billy worked on billing and advertising, and bitched about his arm and being able to do "real work." He had lunch with Kyla when he could, but she'd been working hard and getting an amazing amount done.

Ever since that Abraham guy had showed up two days ago, Kyla had been working like a demon, staying up late and getting up early. She was accomplishing a hell of a lot in a short amount of time, and he was trying to help as best he could by being her model. The night before, she'd gotten him fitted for his pants, and she'd made the fat belt thing and cowhide loincloth for his Khal Drogo costume. He didn't like the idea of strutting in front of a bunch of people for a contest, but he meant it when he said he believed in Kyla, and he wanted her to win.

Besides that, he didn't want that Abraham guy acting as Khal to her Daenerys. That shit was fucking unacceptable.

You're leaving, dude.

He grimaced. He was leaving, true. The rally was in another two weeks. He knew they needed him, especially the younger kids, the new guys. He felt responsible for them, the way the Machinists had been for him when he was younger. But he knew that if he just laid out the truth, they'd understand and fall inline. It wasn't that big a deal. Trevor might talk big, but that was the problem: he was all talk, no game. They'd have the rally.

Then he might come back to Snoqualmie. He wanted to see his grandmother, his uncle.

And you want to see Kyla again.

He wasn't sure how that was going to work, honestly. Would it be a relationship? Did he want that?

He thought about how he'd glided naked into her. Thought about how she made him smile, made him laugh.

Hell yeah, he wanted that. He might be bad at it. He'd never really had a solid relationship before. But she loved him. She'd said so. Maybe he could convince her to be in love with him, too.

Because he was pretty damned sure he was falling in love with her.

He had shut down the shop when his phone started blowing up with texts. He'd been ignoring Mike and Pedro's increasingly frequent and repeated pleas to head back to Vegas. He saw Mike's text. EMERGENCY. PICK THE DAMNED PHONE UP.

He sighed, calling Mike. "What's up?"

"Why haven't you been answering your damned phone?" Mike barked.

"Been busy."

"Yeah, well, get un-busy in a hurry. We need you."

"In Vegas?" Jericho shook his head. "We talked about this, man. I have friends here, people I promised I'd help out."

"Not Vegas," Mike said. "Idaho."

Jericho stopped in his tracks. "Idaho? You mean, at the Rally? I told you I'd be there."

"Not next week. Now."

"What do you mean, now?" Jericho shouted.

"I mean, Trevor's been getting everybody gathered... all the kids especially. He's been talking about changes. He's been talking to the goddamned shops behind our backs!" Jericho couldn't remember when he'd heard Mike this angry. "He's starting a damned coup, dude. He's taking over the Machinists, and he's got bad plans for the kids, I know it. Even my son wants to listen to him. Mike Junior!" He was roaring by this point.

"Hold on a minute," Jericho said, his head spinning. "All right, all right. We can handle this. It's not like he can do anything really. He takes the name, so what?"

"So what? We've got a rep built on these shops," Mike said. "And he's got a bunch of bougie, stupid teens who want to be *Sons of Anarchy* light. Ones who don't have prior records, dumb kids who have rich white parents who are more than willing to bail 'em out of jail. Or kids that cops aren't even going to look at. What do you think's gonna happen if he's got some big plans this weekend?"

Jericho froze.

Oh, Christ.

"All right," Jericho said. "I'll head out."

"Pocatello, Idaho," Mike reminded him. "I'm halfway there. We're following the signs to the camp ground. And get ready to put up a fight."

"I'll try to get there by tomorrow," Jericho said, then hung up.

What the hell am I going to tell Kyla?

He took a deep breath, then headed up the stairs into Kyla's apartment.

She was smiling. "Hey, sexy," she said. "I wanted to do a final fitting on those pants. Then I was thinking I could take a quick break and talk you out of them before I had to work on the Ezio outfit..."

"Kyla, something's come up."

She stopped, her smiling falling. "What's wrong? Are you all right?"

He swallowed hard. "I have to go."

"What?"

"It's my crew," he said. "Some things have come up. The guys are in real trouble. I want to help you, really, I do. But these guys are counting on me."

She bit her lip. "So was I," she said.

He frowned. "This could mean their lives," he said. "They're kids. They're young and stupid. I was like them, back in the day."

She nodded. "When do you have to leave?"

"Tonight."

She blinked, and he saw tears welling up. "When will you be back?"

He paused.

"You don't know, do you?" she said, answering her own question.

He shook his head. 'Ky..."

"It's okay," she said. "I knew what this was. And honestly, I shouldn't have made the Khal outfit. I should've found someone else. That was on me."

"Hey," he said, stroking her cheek, and feeling the pain of it when she stepped away, out of reach of his touch. "I will come back."

"Why, though?" she said. "Those guys need you. Besides, you love being on the road. You love being part of your motorcycle... group of guys you ride with," she said, and he realized that she'd carefully avoided the term "club." She'd remembered.

"I love you, too." His throat felt rough as sandpaper, the words scraping on the way out.

She smiled, but it was lopsided and full of pain. "Love you, too," she said. And he realized: she meant it the way she'd said it before. Loved him – but wasn't necessarily *in* love with him.

He didn't have the time to explain to her what had changed, he realized. Not and still make it to Idaho to avert disaster. And if he did tell her, how much worse would it be? *I'm in love with you, but I still have to leave?*

What kind of a douche said something like that?

He needed to get his head on straight. But he felt like he was getting torn in two.

"It's fine. I promise." Kyla sent him a super-bright smile, which was how he knew she didn't mean it. "This is why we laid out ground rules. So go, do what you need to do. Text when you get there."

"Kyla..."

"I don't have time for drama right now," she said, and her voice was a little sterner even though her eyes were super bright. "I've got my own life, too. You're spread too thin, and I have to take care of myself, remember?"

He should've been taking care of her, he realized. "I'm sorry," he said.

She shook her head with finality. "Don't be. I've got this."

He grimaced. Then he grabbed his stuff, got on his bike, and left.

· ♥ · ♥ · ♥ · ♥ · ♥ ·

Since Jericho had left, Kyla hadn't cried at all. She felt cold, she realized. A little out-of-breath.

She was having a mild panic attack, she realized.

How am I going to get all of this done by deadline?

A small, insidious voice told her it didn't matter. If she didn't make it this time, there were always other conventions, just as Billy had said. This wasn't the be-all and end-all of her costuming career. She could just use what she had, got o the convention that weekend, and enjoy herself. Take the pressure off. If she missed a deadline, big deal. In the larger scheme of things, it didn't matter, right?

She clenched her molars together. But it did matter. *To her.* She was tired of pushing off what she wanted, or pretending she didn't want it. She was tired of putting her wants on the back burner because it wasn't convenient for other people in her life.

She had exactly five days to get all her shit together for this contest. Jericho had left, which meant that there were cars that needed to be fixed. If she went down to the shop and worked for the day, there was absolutely no way she'd be able to get everything done for the convention. And if she didn't find another model for the Khal Drogo, she'd be stuck with a great costume and no entry.

She walked down to the repair shop. Billy was sitting in the office. "Hey there. Where's Jericho?"

"He had to go" Her voice sounded flat to her own ears. "Something came up. Emergency with his biker crew."

"Oh?" Billy sighed. "Must've been bad for him to just leave. Still, you know how he is."

"Yeah. I know how he is."

"It was nice to have his help, though," Billy admitted. "Guy still has the magic touch. We don't have any backlog. You ready to dive in?"

"I've got the convention this weekend," she said.

Billy wasn't listening. Shocker. "Don't worry, it's all easy stuff. Replace a starter, see why somebody's lights aren't working. No big."

"Billy, I can't work this week," she said. "I have to finish those costumes. The convention is this weekend."

He finally looked at her. "You're actually telling me that you're not going to do paying work, so you can..." He made a gesture with his cast, then winced. "...do your convention thing? Are you shitting me right now?"

"No, I'm not," she said. "I'm going to need you to call everybody who's on the docket and tell them that I'll have stuff done by next week, but that's the best I can do."

"No!" Billy stood. "This is bullshit, and you know it, Ky. This is business. We keep our word!"

That did it. She felt like a blood vessel exploded in her brain. "No! *You* keep your word! To *other people!*" she shouted, getting into his space, causing him to back up a surprised step. "I told you no new big projects, no new clients. It's not my fault Jericho didn't keep *his* word and bailed on me. And I told you this was important to me. Summers Child Costumes is important to me!"

"The fuck is Summers Child Costumes?" Billy asked, bewildered.

"That's my costume business," she said, putting her hands on the desk and staring him down. "This is something I've wanted to do for a while."

"And you have been," he said, standing up and putting some anger of his own into his voice. "Nobody's stopping you. But it's not a job, Kyla. It's not a business."

"I'm making money," she said. "It *is* a business."

"No," he said, his eyes narrowing. "The *shop* is a business."

"How would you know?" she spat, all the resentment and anger she'd been building up for the past two years spewing out like lava. "You take vacations, and I cover for you. You get hurt, and I cover for you—"

"It's our business!" he shouted. "And it's not like I broke my arm on purpose, for Christ's sake!"

"How many times have I taken a vacation in the past two years?" she said, her voice coldly furious. "How many times have I covered your shifts or worked early or stayed late? How many times have I backed you when you've wanted to go camping or go somewhere with Lindsay?"

"You could've asked me to cover for you," he pointed out. "Don't make yourself a martyr here!"

"I could've," she said, then took a deep breath. "Remember when I asked you to cover me for a month, so I could go to Comic-Con?"

"Down to San Diego?" He sighed. "That was... We were starting. It was busy. I didn't take any time off then."

"Do you remember?" she ground out.

"They have one every year," he pointed out. "You could've gone this year."

"No, I couldn't," she said. "Because they sold out in a blink. And you said that you were going to ask Lindsay to marry you that week and made it seem like the bigger deal."

"I was planning on it," he said, but she could see him looking away... dodging her accusation. "The ski weekend was a lucky break. No pun intended. Frank's cabin was available, it was the last weekend at Alpental..."

"You always have some excuse," she said. "I love you Billy, but I've let you say that your life and your priorities are more important than mine. I've stayed quiet and been a team player. But I'm sick and tired of it."

She started pacing, forcing herself to calm down.

"I want to be a costumer," she said. "I'm not saying I'm quitting right now. But I want to start scaling back my hours here. I need you to pick up more of the slack."

He frowned. "You make me sound useless."

"You're very competent," she countered. "But you don't do stuff you don't like, and I tend to do it for you. Since you broke your arm, you finally learned the billing system, and you know how to send out the mailings. You can do a lot more than you have been doing."

His face fell. "You can't expect me to do three quarters of the work," he said. "That's not fair, Kyla."

"No, it's not," she said. "But it's also not my problem to make up the difference. We're going to either need to hire a new mechanic or we're going to have to sell the shop."

Billy wouldn't have been more stunned if she'd beaned him with a tire iron. "Dad would be heartbroken!"

"Dad doesn't own the shop anymore," she said. "If we sold it, we could take the money and do what we really want to do. Which isn't necessarily owning the shop," she added gently. "You hate running the business end. I like it, but I don't want to devote all my time to it *and* put in the mechanic work. We need a better solution."

Billy sat down heavily. "Jesus. This is coming out of right field, Ky."

"No, it isn't," she said with a sigh. "You just never noticed, because you need to be hit with a signpost before you finally hear me."

Billy rubbed his face with his good hand. "Well, next time, let me know earlier, okay?" he said, his voice shaking. "I don't think I can take another big shock like this."

She started to walk to the garage. Then she smiled, backing up. "Oh, Billy?"

"Yeah?" he said, his face tired.

"I really was sleeping with Jericho."

"Good one, Kyla," Billy said, chuckling and shaking his head. "I needed that."

And even though her heart broke, she smiled.

· ♥ · ♥ · ♥ · ♥ · ♥ ·

"You did a good job with that," Jericho said to the teen who was trying not to preen over his rebuilt 1981 Honda Hawk.

"I'm just waiting on saving up more money to do the body work," he said. "Took all I had to get parts. But Trevor says that he might have a job for me that'll make me some quick cash."

Jericho gritted his teeth to keep his growl of frustration in. It had taken Jericho ten hours over two days to get to the Palisades Campground by Swan Valley, Idaho, where the Machinists had decided to gather. And in the past five days, bikers had begun to swarm, building up to the weekend's rally. Whatever Trevor was planning, it was something big, and it usually centered on the same things. Quick money. Crew loyalty. And "big changes."

Jericho wanted to punch something. Or, more to the point, some *one*.

"They say there are gonna be like a hundred and fifty people around this week," the kid continued. "Do you think there will really be that many?"

Jericho shrugged, then looked at him. "What's your name again?"

The kid looked at his friends, who seemed impressed. "Darren," he said. "But I was thinking of going by something cooler. Like, maybe Hawk? Like my bike?"

"Darren," Jericho said pointedly, "Do you really want to get into the criminal shit? Join an outlaw motorcycle club?"

Darren took a step back, then looked at his friends, who all exchanged puzzled glances. "Nah. I mean, not really. I just like bikes." He looked sheepish. "But the stuff Trevor's talking about is pretty cool."

"We're not punks," another kid said, with what would've been an impressive sneer if he didn't look all of sixteen years old. "Or pussies. We can handle ourselves."

Jericho suddenly felt ancient. *If I was like this with my Mom*, he thought, *I owe her a better apology.*

"How old are you guys, anyway?"

They let out a chorus of ages, between eighteen and twenty.

"I was seventeen when I left home," Jericho said with a short sigh. "Total gearhead. But I was getting in trouble. Got arrested. Got my best friend into a lot of shit. Finally found the Machinists when I was hanging around a bar in Seattle, in the fucking *parking lot*, because I couldn't sneak in."

The kids laughed. A few looked envious.

"I was lucky I found these guys," Jericho said, his voice turning serious. "I could have fallen in with some deep shit. You want to be running smack or meth? Want to be fucking shooting people, just to prove how tough you are?"

Again, one or two of the boys looked ornery... but he could see the fear, lurking in the depths of their eyes. The others, like Darren, simply looked a little nauseous.

"The Machinists aren't that kind of crew. Not as long as I'm a part of it," he said, his voice sharp. "Spread the word, okay? We're going to have a big talk, and we're going to straighten a few things out."

The kids scattered, and he could see them talking to each other, and then huddling with some other people.

Five days, he thought, groaning. Five days of this bullshit.

I miss Kyla.

He wondered how her costumes were going. He hoped she wasn't trying to juggle the shop as well as sewing. He also wondered, his shoulder muscles tightening, if she'd found someone to replace him.

Maybe that Abraham guy. The dickhead in the boxers, the one who said he was into her. Yeah, I heard that.

He realized his teeth were audibly grinding together, and he forced himself to walk towards a cooler, grabbing a beer. He'd avoided drinking since he'd arrived, because he had to be clear-headed. Now, he just needed something to take the edge off.

You're the one who walked away, he reminded himself. *You had to deal with this. It's important.*

But he'd given his word to Kyla, and that was important to her. And she'd just... accepted it. Like she knew he was going to fail her.

Just like she'd stated in her ground rules: when he left, it was over. And she knew he'd be leaving – and he hadn't countered her. Hadn't even proposed the thought of an alternative. He knew she could take care of herself. *And he let her.*

He looked automatically for Pedro, who was sitting by himself by the Snake River, leaning back with his own beer in his hand. "Helluva view," he said in lieu of a normal greeting. "You should relax, take some of it in. Go riding with us. I was thinking of doing the loop through Salmon and the Lost Trail, follow the rivers. Camp out in the middle somewhere. It's an awesome ride, and it sounds like once whatever goes down with Trevor's shit is done, a lot of people will be ready for some riding instead of talking."

"Trevor is why I haven't been relaxing or riding," Jericho said, his tone brittle. "Have you talked with Mike, or Trevor, since you got here?"

Now Pedro made a face. "Both of 'em. I think we're fine as we are, honestly. Mike's saying make us legit, but honestly, why bring the AMA into it?" He looked at Jericho. "I didn't start the Machinists to fill out a bunch of bullshit paperwork, you know?"

Jericho nodded. "You wouldn't have to be the guy who did the paperwork, though. You could give that to somebody else. Mike's kid seems to have a handle on it. Besides, it's probably better than going outlaw."

"I'm not exactly a choirboy," Pedro pointed out. "A lot of these guys aren't, either... and some of them make *me* look like a saint. We'll lose some regulars if we go all law and order on them."

Jericho sighed. "Maybe we should lose them," he said slowly. "I don't like change, either. But we've got a lot of new guys. A lot of *kids*, dude."

Pedro shrugged. "Free country. And you were younger than most of 'em, and you turned out fine."

Jericho studied his friend. The man had to be in his forties or fifties. Years of riding had made him weathered, like a wrinkled baseball glove, and his black hair was peppered with white. "How old's your kid, P?"

Pedro blinked. "Sunny? She's... what, fourteen?"

"Thought she was in middle school."

He could've sworn he saw his mentor blush. "I think she is." But he didn't sound sure. "I just checked in with her the other day. Says science is a bitch."

The Machinists were Pedro's family. Jericho knew that. Still, he wondered how he felt about being long distance from his kid.

"Maybe we need to change," Jericho said slowly. "Get a little more balance. I love the road, I love bikes, I love builds. But I'm not gonna keep going like this forever."

Pedros' shoulders sank. "Maybe," he said, then looked at Jericho intently. "We were lucky — I was lucky — when I brought you on," Pedro said, and Jericho felt his chest squeeze.

"I was lucky, too," Jericho admitted. "I could've gotten into some really stupid shit. You kept me out of it."

"Yeah, you were lucky," Pedro said, and Jericho laughed. "I think you're good for the crew. You're like our cricket."

"I'm our what?" Jericho said.

Pedro frowned. "The little... with the hat and the umbrella, in that scary ass cartoon." Pedro frowned. "Jimmy cricket."

"Jiminy Cricket?" Jericho started laughing.

"You make sure that the young guys don't get into stupid shit, too," Pedro said gruffly, and Jericho calmed down. "You're a good example. You're a good leader, kid."

Jericho nodded.

"So whatever you decide, I'll back your play," Pedro said. "I trust you."

"That, and you're lazy as shit," Jericho said, his voice shaking.

Pedro laughed. "You got me there."

"Look at you two old men," Trevor said, walking up to them.

Jericho sighed, then stood up to face Trevor, who was looking cocky, with his smirk and swagger. His ever-present side-kick and little brother Connor wasn't there, Jericho noted, and Trevor looked vulnerable without him. He wondered if Trevor was trying to overcompensate as a result. "We need to talk," Jericho said, as Pedro wandered off to grab another beer.

"You been thinking about what we discussed in that hometown of yours?" Trevor looked like he was ready to crawl out of his own skin. "There's like seventy-five people around, and it's a fucking Wednesday. I'm telling you, the Machinists are becoming a force."

"Yeah. It's impressive," Jericho said, rolling his eyes.

Trevor continued. "We keep going at this rate, we can grow to a few thousand in a few years."

"Why?" Jericho asked.

Trevor tilted his head a little, like a confused dog. "Why what?"

"Why do we need or want a thousand people in the club?"

Trevor's eyes widened, then he laughed, but it sounded forced. "Why the hell wouldn't we? The Hell's Angels probably only have two thousand members now. We could be bigger than that, easy."

Jericho felt his gut clench. "I think it's the wrong move, and you know it."

A flare of anger flashed behind Trevor's eyes. "I know it's a big step, but we can handle it," he said, just this side of patronizing. "Trust me. Between Connor and I, we've got it all worked out. And I think you'll find a lot of the new guys are on board."

"I've been talking to the new guys that showed up for the past five days," Jericho said quietly. "And working the email list." A little trick he'd picked up from Kyla.

Trevor's eyes widened.

"I think you're gonna find that they're not quite as down with becoming the next outlaw crew in the U.S. Pedro is backing me on this. And you know Mike has been against your plan from the jump," Jericho said. "I think you're a hell of a rider, and Connor is a frickin' god when it comes to customs. But the rest of it isn't happening. Not with the Machinist name or shops."

Trevor's blue eyes flashed, and his sneer cut deeper. "I told the guys that we were gonna have a little speech before dinner tonight. They're going to be expect me to talk about the stuff we've got planned."

"Yeah, well, you can tell them to enjoy their burgers and shit, and then sit down," Jericho said instead.

Trevor pulled a pack of cigarettes out of his pocket. Jericho noticed that his hand was shaking a little as he lit it. "You don't know about our family, huh? Connor and me?"

Unsure where this was going, Jericho shook his head.

"We were raised with a smaller outlaw group. My grandmother was Helena Weber."

Oh shit, Jericho thought. The Webers? He'd heard talk about them, years ago. Like they tortured people in a sub-basement for selling on their turf, that kind of shit.

"You wanted to turn the Machinists into something like... them?" Jericho said, striving to keep his tone neutral.

"Fuck, no," Trevor said with disgust. "They're old fashioned, just muscle. This is the future."

"Think about it," Trevor said. "We build customs. Custom gas tanks.... with secret compartments. We could run shit in quantity. None of this street corner bullshit, either. We could sell stuff on the dark web. It'd be higher quality. And a whole platoon of clean-cut kids who everyone thinks are just taking a summer on the wild side. We could expand to chop shops. All those other guys, those thugs? They fucking lack *vision*." His eyes gleamed with a desperate eagerness. "I have that vision."

Jericho stood in front of Trevor. "But you don't have the Machinists."

Trevor let out a huff of impatience. "I told you, my family was old school. My Mom was afraid of them. Made 'em promise to leave Connor and me out of it."

Good lookin' out on her part, Jericho thought.

"But before we left, I did learn a few things," Trevor continued. "And one of those things was: if you want to get somebody to do what they don't want to do, you hit 'em where they'll hurt."

Jericho stared in disbelief at Trevor. The guy was maybe five eleven. Without Connor, he wasn't physically imposing at all. "Well, you're welcome to try." Fighting Trevor would be like arm wrestling a hamster.

Trevor shook his head. "You're like a tank, and I'm smarter than that. Besides, I'm not talking about physical pain."

"What the fuck are you talking about?" Jericho snapped.

"That chubby blonde, from the auto shop in Snoqualmie?" Trevor said, in a low, menacing voice. "You seemed real fond of her."

Jericho froze as the implication settled in.

No. Not Kyla.

He reached out, grabbing Trevor by the throat. "What did you *do*?"

Trevor's eyes bulged. "Connor's there," he choked out. "You hurt me, he'll hurt her. If I don't check in..."

"If he hurts her," Jericho said, squeezing, "I'll kill you both."

He dropped Trevor, who fell to his knees. "She'll stay safe as long as you back me up tonight," Trevor said. "And once you get the crew on board, and the shops... well, she'll stay safe, and so will you, as long as you keep your mouth shut. Okay?"

Jericho wanted to kill him, right then and there. But first, he had to make sure Kyla was all right. He called Kyla.

There was no answer.

His next call went to Billy.

"Hey, bro. How are..."

"Shut up," Jericho said. "Go check on Kyla. A biker's gone after her."

"What?"

"Just go!" Jericho yelled, then hung up, hitting Kyla again on speed dial. *Please pick up. Please pick up. Please pick up...*

CHAPTER 10

By Thursday night, Kyla was running on caffeine, adrenalin, and pure, unadulterated frenzy.

"I need somebody brawny," she babbled to Hailey, her cell phone wedged between her shoulder at her chin as she finished carefully tearing off the waxed paper under the pleather pants top seams she'd finally finished. "C'mon. All I need is a decent chest. The pants are long, but I can hem them. You've got to know somebody with pecs! Maybe I can hire a model on Craigslist?"

"By tomorrow?" Hailey asked sarcastically. "Sweetie, even if you say you're looking for a male model on Craigslist, especially one who looks good half-naked, you're going to get weirdos. Why can't you use Adam?"

Adam was their friend Tessa's boyfriend. "He's tall enough, but he's built like a long-distance runner. Comparatively, the guy's a scarecrow, and I don't need a Khal that's wearing suspenders."

Hailey burst out laughing.

"I'm sorry, but I need somebody who looks like they can rip a tree out of the ground with his bare hands."

Hailey made a thoughtful noise. "I might know a security guy who could fit the bill, but he's like five eight."

"That's a lot of hemming, and the crotch wouldn't fit quite right. That's more than an alteration in the damned pleather." Kyla yanked at her hair

"Well, it's not like you're going to find a perfect replacement for Jericho," Hailey said with asperity.

Kyla winced. *Don't I know it.*

Hailey sighed. "Sorry. I didn't mean it like that."

"I know, don't worry about it." Kyla took in a deep breath, then released it, trying to gain some semblance of calm. "Push comes to shove, I'll have Adam wear the *Assassin's Creed* outfit, and have Abraham wear the Drogo – he's tall enough, and built about right, I'd just have to have him dye his beard or wear a wig or something." She paused. "Or I'll just troll biker bars or gyms or something, and find somebody huge who fits the bill."

"Ky, you're sounding kind of crazy. You're not going to do anything extreme, are you?"

"You guys are the ones who told me to go for this," Kyla pointed out. "Now you're telling me I'm going crazy?"

"I'm saying, when you want something or you've been without sleep for too long – or, God forbid, both — you can go off the deep end," Hailey said. "Don't make me pull an intervention, okay?"

"Whatever. Just find me a giant."

"That's it. I'm going to stop by later to make sure you're not embroidering 'all work and no play' over and over on lots of granny squares."

Kyla let out a reluctant laugh and hung up. Hailey had a point. Maybe she was cracking up over this contest. But she'd stood up to Billy, closed the shop, and pinned all her hopes on this. She was going to doing absolutely whatever she had to, to win it.

The fact that you're also going to prove to Jericho that you didn't need his help isn't a factor, huh?

She ignored the sour little voice in her head. That wasn't helpful. She just had to focus.

An hour later, she was cross-eyed and frustrated. None of the girls had found anybody who fit the bill. She never should've fit the costume for Jericho, she realized. A guy who was well over six-foot-tall, and built like a sex god? How was she going to find someone that was going to fit this damned costume? She threw a wad of cloth across the room, gritting her teeth. She wasn't going to go out this way. She just. Was. Not.

There was a knock on the door. She glanced through the peephole. It was a man with a leather jacket and brown hair. She frowned, then quickly opened it.

"Did Hailey send you?"

"What? No." He seemed surprised. "I'm a, um, friend. Of Jericho's." He stepped inside.

That had her heart aching, a quick, surprised slash. "Did he send you?"

"No. Well, not exactly." The mans' face was definitely familiar. And his build. Her brain was too tired to really process at this point.

"Is everything all right?" Kyla asked instead. "Jericho mentioned there was some kind of emergency."

The guy reddened. "Everything is going to be fine."

The way he said it was weird, even if the sentence itself was fine, and she felt her gut twitch, just a little. Of course, she was punchy as hell, and the last thing she'd eaten was half a bag of Reese's miniature peanut butter cups, so she wasn't sure if it was a red flag or just hunger.

"What's your name?" she said. "And how can I help you?"

"Connor," the guy said. "Um, can I use your bathroom?"

She shut the door and was about to point the way when he stopped in the middle of the living room, staring at her couch, where she'd placed some of the costumes. "Is that an *Assassin's Creed* jacket? Ezio Auditore? From the second game?"

"Yes, actually." She gave him a startled smile. "Good eye."

"*Awesome*," he said, leaning closer to inspect the details. "Did you buy that, or make it?"

"I made it." She smiled, relaxing. It was always nice to talk to a fellow geek.

"Really? That's so cool." He was staring at it, at her. "Do you make weapons, too? Like swords and stuff?"

"I focus on fabrics." She sighed. "Um, the bathroom's behind you."

"Oh, that's okay," he said, confusing her. "I just wanted you to shut the door."

Those last words sunk in, and her body clenched in panic. She took a step back.

"Please, don't," he said, and his eyes were woebegone. "Listen, this isn't my idea. I don't want to hurt you or anybody."

She realized from his voice that he was younger than she'd have first pegged him. He let took a deep breath and let out a sigh, his shoulders going up and down. It looked like a mountain shifting.

She froze.

The bikers. This was the man that was with Trevor, the blond guy who had come to talk to Jericho. She remembered thinking the guy had looked like a cliff face. Up close, Connor looked even more imposing, edging into frightening.

"You're with Trevor," she said, earning another surprised glance. "Why are you here? What kind of trouble is Jericho in?" She felt rage building up in her like a volcano.

"You know my brother?" Connor asked, surprised. Then he shook his head. "You don't need to worry about it."

She stepped forward, ignoring his eyes widening. "You don't seem very verbal, so I'm going to be very clear: what the *fuck* are you doing here?"

He blinked. "You're… not scared of me?"

"If you hurt Jericho," she hissed, "you should be scared of *me*."

"Nobody's gonna hurt Jericho," he said. "I'm just here to make sure that he makes the right decisions, that's all."

Her stomach contracted. "You're using me as leverage. Trevor's going to tell him that you have me, so whatever Trevor wants him to do, he'll do. So you don't hurt me."

"My brother has a deal with Jericho. Or is trying to have a deal with him," Connor said. "I'm just going along with my brother, and I swear, I am not going to touch you or do anything to you. I'm just going to hang out here and take a photo of you, okay? To show I'm really here with you."

"A photo? That's it?"

"And... well, maybe, um, tie you up." He still sounded apologetic, and mortified. "But only if it's absolutely necessary, which I'm sure it won't be."

They were using her, she thought. To prove that they "had" her.

Fuck his nice guy attitude, she thought. She was going to make damned sure that he figured out he'd fucked with the wrong woman.

"What do you have? A gun? A knife?"

Connor recoiled. "God, no," he said, his voice rich with disgust.

Now she blinked back. "Then what exactly are you threatening me with?"

He stared, then reddened. "I outweigh you," he muttered. "And I could, um, hurt you pretty easily. Not that I want to. *At all*. Again, this is *not* my idea."

"Spare me," she said sharply.

"No, really," Connor said, glancing around the apartment. "I can just, um, lock you in your room, if you want. Or you can lock yourself in, I mean."

She gritted her teeth, then looked at her phone.

He saw her glance, and sighed. "Sorry," he said, and grabbed it from the counter. Then she watched as he crushed it beneath his heel. "Listen, my family used to be really into this stuff – violence, threats, that stuff — and if my brother didn't need this deal so much..."

She felt a grudging understanding. "Brothers," she said, "can be assholes."

"You're telling me," Connor said beneath his breath. "Here. I've got my phone out."

He took a picture of her glaring. "That really is an impressive costume," he said, as if to mollify her.

The costume.

"You should see what else it has," she said, going into the sewing room. As she expected, he followed her.

She took out her earliest prototypes for Ezio's hidden blades – the ones she'd made special for Hailey the previous year. She grabbed one, turning to him. The "blade" slid out with a fast *snick*.

Connor studied it. "Wicked," he said, with a low whistle. "It'd be more realistic if the ends were, you know, pointed. Why are they flat?"

"Funny you should ask," she said conversationally, before lunging forward.

The tasers at the end snapped to life, and she pressed the contact points to his chest. He made a little "yip!" and fell like a redwood, crashing to the floor.

She sighed. She should call the cops. The guy was huge. She grabbed some zip ties that she had in the closet, and quickly zip-tied his wrists behind him and bound his feet together with sturdy nylon cord. Then she grabbed his wallet.

Connor Weber. He was only eighteen, and in the picture, he wasn't smiling. He'd seemed so excited by the costumes, and he'd reiterated that he wasn't going to hurt her. That wasn't a guarantee – he had made his way into her apartment, after all. But her gut was telling her that he was falling under Trevor's orders. That it was similar to what could've happened to Jericho, if he had joined up with what he'd called one percenters... the truly criminal motorcycle gangs.

She waited in front of Connor until he woke up. He groaned.

"Shit, that hurt," he said, sounding more affronted than in pain. "What'd you hit me with?"

"Taser," she said, watching as he struggled against his bonds. Fortunately, the zip ties and the nylon rope were strong and she'd studied knots since Billy had been in Boy Scouts. "We need to talk. But first, I need to ask you one question."

In that second, he looked like the scared kid he probably was. "What?"

"What size are you?"

· ♥ · ♥ · ♥ · ♥ · ♥ ·

Jericho dialed Kyla frantically, but still got nothing.

"Connor's there," Trevor said with a note of victory. "That'd be that picture I promised." He held it up.

Jericho held his breath, feeling nauseous – until he saw the pic. She was wearing yoga pants and her Punisher T-shirt, her silvery-blonde hair up in a pony-tail on the top of her head with lots of locks spilling out. She also looked purely pissed. At least that was something. Jericho felt hope battle with gut-wrenching fear.

"You don't even have to do anything," Trevor said. "Just tell Mike and Pedro you're with me on this. Then quit the Machinists. Tell 'em you want to settle down and raise chickens or something, whatever. You leave me alone, we'll leave you – and your lady — alone."

The phone chimed. Jericho's muscles tensed.

"It's Connor. Another photo," Trevor said with a bloodless smile. "We don't want to hurt her, Jericho. I just want you to know what you're... *what the hell?*"

Jericho yanked the phone out of his hand and dropped him with a solid punch. He searched Trevor, grabbing a gun from the back of his waistband. He glanced at the photo, but... it looked like Connor, on the floor somehow.

What was going on there?

The phone started ringing, and he answered it. "Connor, this is Jericho," he snarled. "If you fucking touch her, I will kill Trevor and then I will come for you. Do you understand?"

"Jericho?"

Jericho froze. "*Kyla?*"

"Right. Put Trevor on the phone."

Stunned, he put the phone on speaker. "What are you doing to him?" Trevor shouted. "Don't hurt him! Don't…"

"A few things," Jericho heard Kyla's voice through the phone's speaker. "First, we both know that Connor's no longer a minor. He's eighteen and would be tried as an adult for coming into my apartment and threatening me. Both of you would probably serve time for conspiracy to kidnap, and the fact that you're not from Washington would probably suggest it's a federal across-state-lines kinda thing, yeah? I mean, I don't know the exact legal jargon, but that's pretty much how it shakes out."

Trevor went pale, then looked at Jericho. Jericho had no idea, but it sounded scary. And completely plausible.

"We weren't going to kidnap you," Trevor tried.

"Connor sure as hell wasn't here to bring me cookies," Kyla said. "You wanted to threaten me so Jericho would let you turn the Machinists criminal or something, right?"

"Just don't hurt him," Trevor pleaded, tears forming. "Don't hurt Connor."

"I'm not going to. In fact, I like Connor, and I've already figured out how he can make it up to me." She sounded smug. "You, on the other hand, need to stop dragging your brother into this shit because you've got inferiority issues and want to be some kind of gangster. Do you really want Connor going to federal prison? Because I know almost all the police in Snoqualmie and I have a lawyer friend who would make sure you two never see the light of fucking day, Trevor, I promise you that."

She sounded like a cross between a lounge singer and Clint Eastwood, tough and sexy as hell. Even under the circumstances, it was distractingly hot.

"I've also been recording this conversation, which my lawyer friend assures me is legal and admissible," she said, her voice the definition of upbeat confidence. "So put Jericho on the phone, and say goodbye, Trevor."

Trevor was sobbing by this point. Jericho switched off speakerphone. "You okay?" he asked Kyla, still shaken.

"I'm fine. Irritated, but fine."

Relief flooded his system. "This is my fault. I'm sorry."

"It's okay. I got this." It was her hard-as-nails voice. "Just make sure it's handled on your end, all right? That's why you headed out there, isn't it?"

He felt it like a stab wound. *That's why you headed out there.*

That's why he hadn't kept his word. Why he'd left her alone.

Why she was in this mess in the first place.

He'd made it about this. He felt like a caretaker – responsible for the young new recruits, just like he'd once been. He felt it because he owed the Machinists, because they were his family.

But he hadn't carved out a life of his own, and now he was starting to realize what he'd turned his back on.

God, I'm stupid.

"Kyla..." he started, but he heard a commotion.

"*Kyla!*" The sound of a door bursting open, slamming against something. "Where are you? Are you all right?"

"Jesus, Billy! I'm right here!" Kyla said.

There was incoherent yelling. "What happened? Are you... wait, who's *that*?" Billy shouted. "Did he hurt you? Did you call the cops?"

"No, no. That's Connor. I tased him, but don't worry, it's fine."

"He's *tied up!*"

"He's right, I am," a low voice – presumably Connor's – said sheepishly. "Could we take this off yet? Please?"

A woman's startled yelp suddenly added to the chaos. "Kyla, did you tie this guy up?"

"Hailey, it's a long story..."

"Oh, sweetie," Hailey said ruefully. "Not again."

"Not *again*?" Jericho blurted out.

"On the plus side," Kyla said, ignoring his outburst. "Connor will fit the *Assassin's Creed* stuff perfectly!"

Jericho's jaw dropped.

"Good luck with your rally, Jericho," Kyla said brightly, then hung up, leaving him to stare at the phone in awe.

He turned to Trevor, then grabbed him by the back of his collar, dragging him back to the campground, where most of the bikers were gathering. Crowds parted for him like the Red Sea. He threw Trevor near the picnic table where Pedro and Mike were sitting and then gave Trevor's gun to Pedro. They stared at him, bug-eyed.

"This asshole," he said, leaning on Trevor's prone body, "sent his brother to rough up my girlfriend."

Now everyone in earshot fell silent. "You are fucking kidding me," Pedro said, his face colored with disgust.

"All because he wants to turn the Machinists into an outlaw club. Use it to run drugs in custom compartments built by our shops."

"The *fuck* he was," Mike growled.

There were a number of members listening – the ones who were probably waiting for the "big speech" that Trevor had promised. Trevor was still crying from the Connor incident.

Angry, Jericho climbed onto a picnic table, pitching his voice so it was loud enough to reach the crowd. "If it matters, I joined the Machinists because you guys were gearheads. Because you let me be me. I love this club like it was my own blood. But I am sick of this outlaw bullshit. If you want to ride dirty, fucking do it in another club. Or I will personally see to it that you leave this one."

There was a ragged cheer.

"Yeah," Pedro said as Jericho climbed down from the table. "I believe in live and let live, but this is not cool at all."

Mike nodded. "I've been sick of this shit. They can go elsewhere. We'll vote on AMA maybe next year, but this stuff's gotta stop."

Jericho nodded. Then he gestured at Trevor. "I've got to make sure my girl's okay," he said. "And I made her a promise. Can you take care of this trash for me?"

The crew started making noise, and Trevor went pale — paler.

"We got this," Pedro said. "Get out of here. And say hi to your lady for us."

The next day, Kyla was a wreck.

"Where the hell is Abraham?" Kyla said nervously, pacing backstage at OtakuCon.

The contest had just started. She was already dressed as Daenerys, in her Khaleesi outfit of rough leather and pants. Fortunately, it had been done a while ago. She was more worried about how the Khal Drogo costume fit Abraham, who had disappeared into a nearby "dressing area" to get his wig on and get everything together. He'd run late, and she'd come perilously close to killing him.

Connor came off the stage, pulling back the pointed hood of his costume, the exposed skin over his dark brown beard flush. "Did I do okay?" he asked, sounding breathless, his voice pitched a little high.

"You did great," she said. "You really sold it."

And he did. Once he got over a brief bout of stage fright — mainly by being shoved out on stage — he'd "gotten into character" and stalked around the stage like the great assassin himself, including revealing the hidden blades and swirling his cape around.

"You really think so?" he said, obviously eager for approval.

She couldn't help it. She felt her heart soften a little. "I *know* so. There was a lot of cheering. Especially from ladies, I couldn't help but notice."

His cheeks went redder. God, if he could just stay out of that criminal crap, she got the feeling he'd be a really good kid.

"You did awesome, Connor." Mallory said, slim as a blade, her Browncoat trench billowing as she put her hands in her pockets. She looked great, too. "I think we've got a good shot at winning this, Ky."

Kyla swallowed nervously. "I think that Hailey's Megara was a hit," she said. "And Rachel's obviously beautiful, but I don't think as many people are as familiar with the Liliana character here as they are at other conventions."

Rachel held out her hands, looking every inch a lethal yet luscious goth character. "I like *Magic: The Gathering*, and I think a lot of people are familiar with the game," she said.

"Even if they aren't," Hailey added, "I think the combo of sexy, magical, and evil works."

"Thank you," Rachel said, with a little bow.

If Connor went any redder, he'd turn into a pomegranate.

"Where *is* Abraham?" Kyla repeated, now starting to feel nervous. "They're going to call us up any minute!"

The couples were already showing off. They were supposed to be two of the last ones. She'd decided to make Abraham play Khal Drogo because, while Connor might actually fit the outfit better, she just felt weird being a "couple" and trying to sell romance with a guy who had just the day before been thinking of imprisoning her in her own house, and now was acting like a goofy sidekick who desperately wanted to join their Justice League.

Abraham, on the other hand, made it clear that he'd be happy to act romantically involved with her.

She sighed. Unfortunately, she wasn't interested.

Damn that Jericho.

She knew why he'd left. And after seeing Connor, she couldn't disagree with him. But she wished, just once, that a man would inconvenience himself for her. That when a man said that he'd help, he'd keep his word. She wanted someone to put her first.

But until then, she thought, shoulders squared, she'd just have to take care of it herself.

"Summers Child Costumes! Couples cosplay — you're up!" a woman with a headset said, gesturing to the stage.

Looking behind her, she growled. "Tell Abraham to get his ass out here," she said to Hailey, then strode across the stage herself.

She felt a little self-conscious. She wasn't graceful like Rachel, or built like a sex goddess like Hailey. She knew she was rounded where it wasn't considered sexy to be round, and she certainly wasn't the petite little waif that people wanted to see when they thought of Daeneyrs Stormborn. She saw people staring at her, alone, and felt a crushing bout of doubt.

Then she planted her feet in her leather boots, put her hands on her hips, and stared them all down.

Behold. I am Kyla Summers, she thought haughtily. *Queen of No Fucks Given, Slayer of Entitled Douchebaggery, First of Her Name*. Silently, she dared any of them to say otherwise.

Suddenly, she heard a low growl, and she spun.

"Jericho," she breathed.

He was dressed in full Khal splendor: the wide wedding belt she'd made with the horse details, the claw-like paint down his pecs, the guyliner making his eyes even more dramatic. The beard, the blades, the whole nine yards.

He looked powerfully edible. She could almost hear the collective sigh from the women in the crowd.

"*Yer jalan atthirari anni!*" he said loudly and clearly.

She gaped at him as most of the audience gasped and hooted with approval. He'd just said, in pitch-perfect Dothraki, Khal Drogo's famed endearment for his wife: *Moon of my life.*

She couldn't help it. Her heart melted in a puddle.

"*Shekh ma shieraki anni,*" she replied back. *My sun and stars.*

And in a second, he took two long strides, picked her up, and kissed her.

The crowd went nuts, but she could barely hear it, because her mind had exploded in longing and love and simple, sheer overwhelm.

He put her down, still kissing her. Then he pulled back, stroking her cheek, staring into her eyes.

"You came," she murmured, still in shock. "You made it in time."

"I'm sorry," he said, at almost the same time. "I'll always be there for you from now on. Always."

"It's..."

"It's not all right," he said. "Because I love you. I'm *in* love with you. And I'm not going anywhere."

The crowd cheered again, and she realized: he'd just made a full-on declaration in front of the entire contest crowd. The announcer sighed.

They made their way backstage. Rachel was dabbing at tears, while Hailey was hooting like a train whistle. Abraham was nodding in understanding, still in his street clothes.

"Your guy put up a persuasive argument before I could get the outfit on," he said, with a quicksilver grin. "If you ever get tired of him, let me know."

Before Jericho could growl again, she threw her arms around his waist. "I'm never getting tired of him," she said. "Because I'm in love with him, too."

Jericho looked down at her, eyes shining.

They waited for the judges' deliberations. She spent most of the time in Jericho's arms. He seemed to want to reassure himself that she was all right. Abraham joked with Hailey and Rachel. Connor was talking with some of the other contestants, several of whom were his age. She saw him talking animatedly to some guys dressed in *Fallout 4* power armor suits they'd designed themselves. She got the feeling that he'd found a group of his own, one that addressed his hidden geeky side, and it warmed her heart.

"And now, the winner of the overall costume contest is..." she heard, and clasped Jericho's hand tightly.

"...*Summers Child Costumes!*"

· ♥ · ♥ · ♥ · ♥ · ♥ ·

Later that night, Jericho and Kyla sat in Kyla's apartment. Connor was settled in at Abraham's, waiting for his brother to arrive. Rachel and Hailey were celebrating and showing off video to Cressida, who couldn't attend because of her agoraphobia. Jericho was exhausted from the ten hour ride he'd endured, rushing to get back to Kyla, and the day at the Con. But even exhausted, he couldn't help but feel the surprised bursts of happiness in his chest every time he saw Kyla near him, wearing her boy shorts and Punisher t-shirt, her face glowing with quiet joy.

She moseyed over to the couch, straddling him. "I'm so glad you came back," she said, pressing a long kiss against his mouth.

"I swear, I'm never gonna leave you again," he swore, kissing down her throat, savoring the sound of her gasp.

"It's okay. I know how much it means to you to mentor kids, especially boys the age you were," she said, stroking his chest and resting her forehead against his. "As long as you let me know, I'm more than happy to let you go. I know you'll come back."

"Always," he breathed, gently nipping at her lower lip. "You're one of my best friends. You are the best sex I've ever had. I always loved you. And as soon as I saw you again, it was like I'd been waiting for you. I just didn't put it together."

"I knew," she said smugly, and he laughed. "I'm just amazed that you finally did figure it out."

"Because I have testicles," he mocked.

"Because you have testicles," she agreed, then nudged the juncture of her thighs against his cock. "Although I suppose they're very nice testicles."

He felt himself harden and lengthen, and reached under her shirt, cupping one of the globes of her breast. "You also have some very nice qualities," he agreed.

They were laughing as they kissed – and that's when Billy walked in.

"So did you win... *what the hell is going on here?*"

Kyla made a "meep!" noise, and almost pulverized him trying to vault off of him. Jericho made an answering "oof," but held her close.

"It's pretty much what it looks like," Jericho said, holding tight as Kyla wiggled like crazy.

Billy stared, his mouth agape, then made a half-hearted, suspicious laugh. "You're... kidding. Right?" He asked almost desperately.

"No," Jericho said. "Sorry, dude. I'm in love with your sister."

Billy stared, going from Kyla to Jericho, then back again. "You're in love with Ky?" he repeated, as if it might somehow come out differently.

"'Fraid so," Jericho said. "And she loves me too."

"Yup," she said, hiding underneath his chin and snuggling closer.

Billy shook his head. "Okay, no. No. I refuse to accept this. I am going to go home, drink large quantities of beer, until all memory of this moment is bludgeoned to death."

Jericho laughed. Even Kyla snickered.

"And if you're gonna keep doing this, a few thing," Billy said. He pointed at Jericho. "If you hurt her, I'll kill you."

"I respect that," Jericho agreed.

Billy then pointed at Kyla. "If I hear any hanky-pank or see any weirdness, I will..."

"You'll do what?" Kyla said. "Remember, I walked in on you and Lindsay in that laundry basket."

He went scarlet. "Just don't let me see or hear anything!" Billy roared, then promptly retreated, leaving them both laughing.

"A laundry basket, huh?" Jericho said. "How the hell does *that* work?"

She smiled, then got up and locked the door. "I'm not sure," she said. "But I think we can figure out something better."

EPILOGUE

"Don't be nervous," Kyla reassured him. "It'll be fine."

It was June. It had been almost a month since he'd talked to his mother, and now Jericho took Kyla over to his family's house in Carnation. They rode on the back of his bike, and he loved the feel of her arms around his waist and her thighs pressing against his hips. He needed all the positive, happy emotions he could get at this point, because going to see his family after all of these years was definitely making him nervous.

He was nervous as hell and glad that Kyla was coming with him. She'd always been good at helping him get out of his own head, even when he was a pissed-off kid. Now, she was like a balm to his soul.

She'd insisted that they bring something. She'd run out and grabbed some cake pops from a nearby bakery so they weren't coming empty-handed. She'd also grabbed a toy for his brother, Sam, a big wooden puzzle of a dinosaur.

He knew she'd be a great girlfriend. And when she was ready for it, he got the feeling she'd make one hell of a wife, he thought with a grin.

Jericho shifted his focus back to the present. There were several cars there already. His family had already arrived.

He felt Kyla reach out for his hand, giving it a squeeze. He squeezed back, nudging her. "I'm so glad you're coming with me," he breathed, kissing her gently, nibbling at her lips. "You always make me feel better."

She smiled. "I've got your back, babe. Always."

At that moment, the door opened. His uncle Sid looked just the same — inky hair like his own, that burnished copper skin from plenty of time spent outdoors. He wore a plaid shirt and a pair of jeans. Uncle Sid came out with another man, a good-looking guy with silver-streaked hair, a button-down shirt, and a pair of khakis.

"There you are!" Sid came up to him, giving him a big, exuberant hug. Jericho patted his back in return. Then Sid pulled back, his eyes glassy with unshed tears. He cleared his throat. "Isn't the house great? They bought it about four years ago, before real estate went so crazy over here on the east side. Everything's a bedroom community of Seattle anymore," his uncle enthused. Of course, his uncle was generally enthusiastic, Jericho remembered, but this was over the top even for him. He was rambling.

Maybe he was nervous, too. That helped a tiny bit, that Jericho wasn't the only one who thought all this was nerve-racking.

"This is my husband, Paul," his uncle said with a grin. Paul offered Jericho a shy smile and shook his hand.

Taking his uncle's cue, he shifted over to Kyla. "This is Kyla Summers. She's my girlfriend."

Sid narrowed his eyes, studying her. "Don't I know you?"

Jericho nodded as Kyla smiled. "Her brother's my best friend. I've known the whole family for years."

"That's sweet," his uncle said, giving her a hug. "I'm so glad you could come, Kyla. Come on in, meet the family." With that, he guided her inside, Jericho trailing behind.

His stepfather, Gary, was sitting on a gray leather couch, talking with his grandmother. His grandmother's eyes watered and she stood. "Jericho," she said, choking up as she reached out her hands.

She had to be in her seventies now, but young seventies, he thought as he gave her a hug and felt his own throat clog with emotion. Now, she looked a bit older, a bit heavier, her face more heavily lined. But her brown eyes still twinkled the way he remembered. Her hair was snow white and pulled back in a braid. She was wearing a pair of jeans and a nice grayish-green shirt, the color of river water.

She smiled at him. Then she lightly smacked him on the shoulder. "Where the hell have you been?"

"Ma!" his mother yelled out from down the hall, scandalized. "What did we talk about?"

He heard the peal of his little brother's laughter and what sounded like splashing.

"She's giving your brother a bath," his grandmother said, ignoring his mother's admonishment with a wave of her hand. "I'm just saying, it's been ten years..."

"Nine," he corrected gently.

"*Years* since you even made contact. You gonna disappear again?"

It seemed like everybody else in the room — his stepfather, Gary, his uncle, his uncle's husband — held their breath and waited with a weighted pause.

He gave her a hug. "No, Gram," he said. "I'm settling down here, in Snoqualmie. I'm going to be working with the Summers, buying into their auto shop. I was thinking of doing some mentoring with kids who like auto stuff, and motorcycles. I was even thinking of helping with that kind of thing around the tribe, maybe, if they're interested."

Her eyes went wide, as did her smile.

"Anyway," he muttered, "I promise: I'm not going to disappear."

Before she could continue talking, laughter burst out again, then suddenly a small, wet, naked person bolted from the hallway and toward the still-open front door. Acting on instinct, Jericho moved, stepping in front of the streaking little guy before he could make a full-on break for freedom.

Sam giggled wildly, trying to get around him.

"Dude," Jericho said, shaking his head and grinning. "You need clothes."

Gary grabbed the boy as his mother emerged, her clothes sopping wet.

"I swear, Jericho, you were a snap compared to this little escape artist," she said, her expression frazzled.

Everyone laughed, releasing the earlier tension. "He's quite the nudist, too," Gary said, trying to keep his grip on the soapy, slick child.

"Oh, Jericho was a pain in the ass, too," his grandmother assured her. "But it's easier to wrangle a kid when you're twenty than when you're forty."

"Ass!" Sam repeated with glee.

"Ma," his mother warned. "You know he echoes everything these days."

"Psh." His grandmother looked unconcerned, even as her eyes twinkled. Jericho got the feeling that this was a conversation they had often.

They all settled into conversation. The rest of the evening went by in a pleasant blur of food, conversation, and ease.

Later that night, he held Kyla tight, under the summer stars out in the front yard of his Mom's house.

"You okay?" she asked, looking up at him.

He stood by his family, by his bike, by his woman. It was going to be all right. He knew that, no matter where he went, he was rooted here now. He felt something start to release in his chest... something new. Something wonderful.

"I'm okay," he said, and kissed her. "And when I'm with you, I'm even better. Because you're my home."

Thank you so much for reading Kyla and Jericho's story!

Want to keep hanging out with the crowd at Frost Fandoms? Next up: Tessa's best friend Ani's story, *What Happens at Con*. You won't believe who she winds up with!

A Note from Cathy

Hi!

Thank you so much for reading *Game of Hearts*. The Fandom Hearts series is all about finding the things you're passionate about — the things you're geeky about — and going all in. I loved writing this series, and I hope you enjoy reading it just as much. The series is complete (I think? For now?

Although some of those secondary characters have been nudging at me!) and each book can be read as a stand-alone, although they can be enjoyed in chronological

series order for the full experience. And there are other series to enjoy if you're looking for more fun, geeky love stories!

If you do enjoy the book, please take a minute to write a review of this on Amazon and Goodreads. Reviews make a huge difference in an author being discovered in book searches and shared with other readers!

And if you'd like to connect with me, I love hearing from readers! You can stop by www.CathyYardley.com to email me, or visit me on social media. Or join my Facebook readers group, Can't Yardley Wait, to see early reveals, exclusive content, and a lot of shenanigans with a very fun
group.

Enjoy!

Cathy

ABOUT AUTHOr

Cathy Yardley writes fun, geeky, and diverse characters who believe that underdogs can make good and sometimes being a little wrong is just right.

She likes writing about quirky, crazy adventures, because she's had plenty of her own: she had her own army in the Society of Creative Anachronism; she's spent a New Year's on a 3-day solitary vision quest in the Mojave Desert; she had VIP access to the Viper Room in Los Angeles.

Now, she spends her time writing in the wilds of Eastern Washington, trying to prevent her son from learning the truth of any of said adventures, and riding herd on her two dogs (and one husband.)

Want to make sure you never miss a release? For news about future titles, sneak peeks, and other fun stuff, please sign up for Cathy's newsletter here.

Let's Get Social!

Hang out in Cathy's Facebook group, Can't Yardley Wait

Talk to Cathy on Twitter

See silly stuff from Cathy's life on Instagram

Never miss a release! Follow on Amazon

Don't miss a sale — follow on BookBub

ALSO BY

THE PONTO BEACH REUNION SERIES

Love, Comment Subscribe

Gouda Friends

Ex Appeal

THE FANDOM HEART SERIES

Level Up

Hooked

One True Pairing

CATHY YARDLEY

Game of Hearts

What Happens at Con

Ms. Behave

Playing Doctor

Ship of Fools

SMARTYPANTS ROMANCE

Prose Before Bros

STAND ALONE TITLES

The Surfer Solution

Guilty Pleasures

Jack & Jilted

Baby, It's Cold Outside

Printed in Great Britain
by Amazon